POINT BLANK

SANDRA ROBBINS

HARLEQUIN® LOVE INSPIRED® SUSPENSE

LOVE INSPIRED BOOKS

Recycling programs for this product may not exist in your area.

ISBN-13: 978-0-373-45729-8

Point Blank

Copyright © 2017 by Sandra Robbins

www.Harlequin.com

Printed in U.S.A.

Brethren, I count not myself to have apprehended:
but this one thing I do, forgetting those things
which are behind, and reaching forth unto those things
which are before, I press toward the mark for
the prize of the high calling of God in Christ Jesus.
—Philippians 3:13-14

To Marti,
for introducing me to the world of mounted archery.

ONE

Hannah felt the gun pressed to her back the minute she returned the nozzle to the gas pump. She stiffened and glanced over her shoulder. A man, his face obscured by a black hoodie, nudged her with the gun again.

"Don't make a sound, lady, or it will be your last." Out of the corner of her eye, she saw him reach out with his left hand and open the driver's door. "Get in and crawl over the console to the floor in front of the passenger seat," he hissed.

Hannah's body stiffened, but her legs went so weak that they threatened to collapse. She reached out and grabbed the top of the door to keep from falling. The thought kept running through her mind that this couldn't really be happening to her. Robberies and car jackings were supposed to happen to other people—strangers she heard about on the news. But then the terrible realization hit her that this time she was the one people might hear about tomorrow.

As the reality of her situation soaked in, a new fear

swept through her. She was a single mother, with no family other than her daughter. What would become of Faith if something happened to Hannah? She had to do everything she could to make it out of this encounter alive. The problem was she didn't know whether her safest choice was to obey her attacker or scream for help.

Still gripping the door, she took a deep breath and spoke in a shaky voice. "P-please, take m-my car. Take m-my money. Just let me go."

He laughed, and this time he pressed the gun even harder. "Get in now," he ordered.

Hannah cast a terrified glance toward Bart's Stop and Shop, the convenience store where she always bought gas for her car, and prayed that Bart was watching his security cameras.

"I said get in the car!" the man growled.

Before she could respond, the store's door opened, and Bart stepped outside. "What's going on out here?" he yelled.

The attacker answered with a shot that struck the pavement a few feet from where Bart stood. He turned and ran back into the store, and her assailant muttered something that she couldn't understand before he gave her a hard shove. She fell into the car and then scrambled over the console as he had ordered until she was on her knees on the floorboard of the passenger side with her upper body on the seat. The car door slammed, and they roared from the parking lot.

As they sped down the street, Hannah started to

push up. "Don't move!" the man shouted. "I'll tell you when you can get up."

"Why are you doing this?" Hannah cried. "You can have my car, just let me out."

He shook his head and chuckled. "Be quiet, and this will all be over before you know it."

His words struck a warning bell in her mind. All be over? What did he mean? She shuddered at the thought that she might be living the last few minutes of her life.

A pain stabbed her heart, and a tear rolled down her cheek at the thought of Faith, her little girl who'd already lost a father. It wasn't fair for her to grow up without her mother, too. Perhaps she could reason with her abductor.

"Mister, I don't know who you are or why you're doing this. I have a daughter who needs me. I'm the only one she has in this world. Please, if you have any compassion in your heart, let me go."

Hannah waited for him to respond, but his only answer was a grunt as he accelerated the car.

She waited a few seconds for him to say something. When he didn't, she raised her head just enough to look at him and tried again. "If you want money, I'll give it to you. I don't have much, but you can have it all if you'll just let me out of the car."

This time his answer was a swift slap to the face. "Shut your mouth!" he yelled. "I don't care about your daughter or your money or anything else."

She pressed her hand to the stinging spot on her face and stared up at him. "Then why are you doing this? I don't know you, do I? You sound as if you have some kind of grudge against me."

His sinister laugh made her skin prickle. "Grudge? I guess you could call it that. All you need to know is that it's payback time."

"Payback for what?"

"I'll tell you in my own time. For now, stay down on the floorboard and keep your mouth shut."

Hannah started to protest, but she changed her mind when one of his hands drifted from the steering wheel and clutched the gun that lay in his lap. If she provoked him further, he might decide to end her life right now. She had to bide her time and wait for an opportunity to escape. She didn't know how or when or even if that would ever be, but she needed to watch and take advantage of the first opportunity she had to get away from this man.

She glanced at him once more before she leaned her head against the car seat and looked up through the moon roof. Vivid colors of the afternoon sunset reminded her that she was never alone. She closed her eyes and sent a silent prayer to God.

Give me strength, Lord, to face what is to come. If I should die tonight, I pray that You would please take care of Faith. I ask You to provide people who will love her and give her a good home.

The prayer broke her heart. She couldn't stand to think about another woman tucking her child into bed at night, helping her with homework or doing any of the many tasks a mother performed. But she had just placed Faith's future in God's hands. All she could do now was wait and see what happened.

* * *

Sheriff Ben Whitman let his gaze drift over the bumper-to-bumper traffic inching along the highway through the middle of the small mountain town where he'd grown up. Things certainly had changed here since he was a boy. A town that had once been a wide spot in the road on a route into the Smoky Mountain National Park had now become one of the top tourist attractions in the Smokies.

Throngs of tourists showed up year-round, and souvenir shops and amusement attractions now lined the thoroughfare through the town. On nights like this, the streets were packed. Tourists who were fortunate enough to have found a parking place were ambling from one shop to another while the slow-moving cars hovered like vultures waiting to pounce on the first parking space available. He had lost count of how many fender benders they'd answered calls for this week because two vehicles vied for the same open spot.

Ben glanced over at Deputy Luke Conrad, who was driving the police car, and sighed. "Looks like a big night for the merchants."

Luke nodded. "Yeah. How about if I turn right up here at the next stoplight and get out of this traffic jam?"

"Sounds good," Ben responded. "If we don't, we may find ourselves boxed in somewhere if we get a call."

Luke turned on the car's blinking lights and maneuvered onto the side road that led to a street that ran parallel to the highway. Once they were out of the crowd, Luke smiled. "Where to now?"

Ben was about to answer when the radio crackled with a message from dispatch. "Abduction of a female identified as Hannah Riley at gunpoint from Bart's Stop and Shop. Victim last seen being forced into her white SUV, headed toward Wears Valley. Suspect armed and dangerous."

Luke jerked his head around and stared at Ben. "Does the Hannah Riley you know have a white SUV?"

Ben's heart had begun to pound at the message. All he could do was nod. He'd just seen Hannah that morning when he stopped by her ranch to check on her and Faith. She'd looked happy and was practicing her archery skills in the backyard. How could this have happened to her of all people?

He pushed his fears for his friend away, knowing he had a job to do. There had been a woman taken against her will, and they had to try to stop the culprit. He only hoped they were in time to save her life.

He spoke into his shoulder mic. "Copy that. Unit 1 in pursuit toward Wears Valley. Request backup."

"Ten-four, Unit 1. Backup on the way."

Ben gritted his teeth and exhaled. "Light 'em up, Luke!"

He'd no sooner spoken the words than Luke turned on the blue lights, and they were racing toward the highway that led to Wears Valley. Questions poured through his mind as they sped down the highway.

Did the attacker intend to kill his victim, or did he just want her car? If he'd wanted the vehicle, why did he force the woman to go with him? The possible answers to those questions made his stomach roil.

They passed the road that turned off and circled back to the national park entrance. What if the abductor had taken that turn? For a moment Ben debated telling Luke to go back and turn onto that road, but he didn't. Even at this time of late afternoon, there would still be tourists at the scenic stops along that route, and a speeding car would draw attention. If the suspect was smart, he would probably have made the decision to continue on the road on which they were traveling.

One thing bothered him, though. There were lots of turnoffs along this highway that led into the mountains with its many trails. They didn't have the time or manpower to efficiently search every one. If the kidnapper took one of those, he and his victim would be lost to them. If he decided to dispose of his victim, her body might never be found in that wilderness. They had to get to her in time.

Ben leaned forward and stared out the windshield in hopes of catching a glimpse of the vehicle. After a few minutes, he was about to think he'd made the wrong choice to stay on this road when he spotted a car in the distance. It was barely a speck on the horizon, but it looked like it was white.

He held his breath as Luke accelerated and shortened the distance between the two cars. "That's a white SUV!" Luke said as he pulled even closer.

Ben's heart seemed to jump into his throat as they neared the car. All hopes that there might have been a mistake in identifying the victim—that it might be someone other than Hannah—died when he caught sight of the familiar license plate on the back of the car. Hannah hadn't been content to settle for one of the regular state license plates and had bought one of the specialty plates the state offered. Hers was one issued to University of Tennessee supporters and personalized with the words VOLS FAN as a tribute to the football team she followed with a passion.

He had to face the fact that he'd been trying to deny ever since getting the call. Hannah was in jeopardy. But where was she? He could see the outline of a man's head behind the steering wheel, but there was no sign of anyone with him. Were they too late? Had he already disposed of her?

Luke switched on the siren as they bore down on the car, and Ben pulled his gun from its holster. The deepening afternoon shadows lit up as the flashing lights reflected across the area. The kidnapper had to have heard the sound, but his response was to increase his speed. Luke pressed down on the accelerator, and they sped after the car.

Suddenly Ben heard a sharp crack as a bullet whizzed past the driver's window of the squad car. Luke was too experienced to startle or swerve. Instead he frowned and pulled closer to the fleeing SUV. "You're not getting away from me," he muttered as another shot pinged on the bumper of the car.

Ben rolled down his window and hesitated before sending an answering shot. What if his aim wasn't true? He could shoot Hannah if she was still in that car, or he could cause the car to wreck, which might leave her dead or injured.

He'd been in similar situations before, but never in a circumstance like this. Hannah wasn't just another victim whose life had been placed in danger. This was his friend. He'd known her since she'd come to live with her grandfather in the Smokies after she graduated from college. He'd also become friends with her late husband, and he was godfather to her daughter. How could he risk her life? On the other hand, who knew what she would face at her abductor's hands if he allowed them to get away?

Another shot whistled past, and he took a deep breath as his decision was made. "Hold the car steady, Luke," he said as he stuck his arm out the window and aimed for one of the back tires of the car.

For a moment he closed his eyes and prayed. *Make my shot count, Lord.*

Then he opened his eyes, refocused his aim and fired at Hannah's SUV.

Hannah, her hands covering her head, crouched on the floorboard of the car. She heard the sirens behind them and saw the reflection of the flashing lights in the mirror on the side of her vehicle. Could Ben be in that squad car? She had no doubt he would come if he knew what had happened to her. —

Suddenly she didn't have any fear. God had answered her prayer already. She had asked him to send Faith to someone who loved her, and now she knew who that would be. Ben had been a dear friend to her for years, and he loved her daughter as if she were his own. If she was to die today, she knew that Ben would see that Faith was cared for.

No sooner had the thought flashed in her mind than she saw her abductor raise his hand with the gun. She sucked in her breath and waited for him to shoot her. Instead he rolled down the window and fired at the police car. The sirens and lights continued to follow them. Then he shot again.

She lost count of how many times he shot, but she was afraid that sooner or later he would disable his target. Then she heard an answering shot as it hit the back of her car. The police were answering the fire!

She crouched even farther and tried to roll into a fetal position, but there was barely enough room on the floorboard to get her head below the seat. Another shot hit the back of the car, and she bit down on her lip to keep from crying out.

Her kidnapper cursed under his breath and fired toward the car again. Almost immediately there was the sound of an answering bullet striking its target, and her car ran onto the shoulder before it careened back onto the highway. She knew right away that the pursuing officer's bullet had struck one of the back tires. The relief she felt at knowing someone was trying to help her died quickly as the car began to swerve out of control back and forth across the highway. Her abductor wouldn't be able to get away with her…but they seemed to be headed for a crash that could kill them both.

"No!" Her abductor yelled and grabbed the steering wheel with both hands as he struggled to gain control of the car.

His gun dropped from his hand and landed on the car's console. Before he could react, Hannah grabbed the gun and pointed at him. "Stop this car!" she yelled.

He turned his head toward her, and the hoodie slipped back on his head. For the first time she saw his eyes, and she recoiled at the pure hatred in them. He grasped the steering wheel with one hand and gritted his teeth as he reached over and hit her in the jaw with his fist.

The force of the blow sent her head spiraling back against the door. The impact blinded her for a moment, but she was determined not to let him wrest the gun from her hand. She placed her finger around the trigger and tightened her grip on the pistol.

"Stop this car!" she ordered.

His lips curled into a sneer, and he pulled one hand away from the steering wheel. He doubled it into a fist and snarled at her. "Give me that gun before I make you sorrier than you already are!"

Hannah knew it was now or never. She could cower on the floorboard and let him kill her, or she could fight for her life. If she shot him, the car would probably wreck and she might be killed. On the other hand, if he gained control of the gun, she could still be killed— and he'd probably try to make her death as painful as possible. She had the choice, and she wasn't about to give the gun to him.

Gritting her teeth, she wrapped both hands around the gun, aimed at him and fired. The driver's window shattered at the impact, and he screamed. "You crazy woman, what do you think you're doing?"

He reached toward her again. This time his fingers wrapped around the gun and jerked it from her hand. Determined that she wouldn't give up, she clawed at his hands in an effort to get the weapon back. For the first time she noticed that he wore disposable gloves, and she dug her nails into them.

With a cry of rage, he pulled free of her and aimed the gun at her. Before he could fire, another shot from the police car struck the other back tire. The car veered toward the right and hit the loose gravel on the shoulder of the road. Hannah screamed as the car hurtled down the embankment, crashed through a fence and slammed nose-first into a tree. Her last conscious thought was that she hoped the police got to them in time to save her life.

Ben watched in horror as Hannah's SUV careened off the road and became airborne for a moment before it crashed. Luke pulled the squad car to a stop on the side of the road, and they both jumped out. In the distance sirens screamed the approach of another police car.

Please let her be all right. Please let her be all right.

The prayer echoed over and over in Ben's head as he and Luke ran toward the SUV that had smoke pouring from underneath it. He still couldn't see Hannah's head, and the fear that he was about to find her body inside the car that had folded like an accordion upon impact against the tree filled his mind.

He'd already unholstered his gun, and Luke pulled

his out as the driver's door of the wrecked car opened. A man wearing dark jeans and a black hoodie jumped out and spun to face them. He had a gun in his hand.

"Put the gun down!" Ben yelled.

The man answered with a shot that kicked up dirt a few feet away from him. Ben didn't slow as he returned fire. The man ducked behind the open door to gain cover and fired again. This time the shot hit near Luke's feet.

Ben and Luke both dived for cover behind the car and pressed their bodies against the hatch. "You can't escape!" Ben called out. "Don't add more charges to those you're already facing."

Two bullets in quick succession blazed past Ben's hiding place, and then he heard movement. He raised up enough to see the man running toward the forest at the back of the field. "I'm on it!" Luke called out as he jumped to his feet. "You stay here and see if Hannah's inside."

Before Ben could stop him, Luke took off in pursuit of the fleeing man. The sheriff ran around to the passenger side of the car and jerked the door open. His heart plummeted to the pit of his stomach when he saw Hannah crouched on the floorboard with her head resting on the seat. The windshield's shattered glass covered her and the seat. She didn't move as he touched her arm.

Blood poured down the side of her face from a cut at her hairline, and he raked the fragments of glass off the top of her head. He held his breath as he placed his fingers on her neck. The steady thump of her pulse sent a wave of relief coursing through him.

Ben turned his face to his shoulder mic. "Unit 1. Officer in pursuit of fleeing suspect. The victim is secure, but unconscious and in need of medical attention. Requesting more backup and an ambulance on highway at Wears Valley."

"Ten-four," Clara the dispatcher replied. "Ambulance on the way. More backup en route."

Ben wanted to examine Hannah more thoroughly to see if he could detect any other injuries, but with the risk of spinal injuries, he was afraid to move her. He leaned over and whispered to her in hopes that she could hear him. "Hannah, it's Ben. I'm here. Everything's going to be all right. You're safe now, and help is on the way."

She stirred, and he held his breath as she lifted her head and stared up at him. "Ben," she whispered. "Is it all over?"

He squatted and returned her gaze. "The guy who kidnapped you ran off, but Luke is after him. The important thing right now is whether you're okay. Are you hurting anywhere?"

She lifted her hand to her forehead, frowned as she touched the blood and pulled her hand away to stare at it. "My head hurts, but I think I'm okay otherwise."

She started to push up, but he put a hand on her and restrained her. "Don't move. I want the EMTs to examine you first. Just try to relax until they get here."

Tears pooled in her eyes, and the muscles in her throat constricted as she swallowed. "I think he really meant to kill me. I was so scared, Ben. Not for myself, but for Faith. She has no other family than me, and I prayed that God would give her a family to love her. Then I thought of you, and I knew you would never let anything happen to her."

His chest tightened, and he took a deep breath. "You know I love Faith like she's my own daughter. As long as I'm alive, I'll be there to take care of her and you, too."

"You're a good friend, Ben," she whispered as she let her head drop back to the seat.

Ben started to say something else, but the sirens that had been wailing in the distance had now grown louder. He glanced up to see an ambulance and a squad car, their emergency lights flashing, stop beside his patrol car on the highway. Joe Collins, and another EMT who Ben hadn't seen before, jumped from the ambulance and ran with the backup officers to where he stood.

"In here!" he called out to Joe.

He backed away as the paramedics swooped in to examine Hannah, then turned to the two deputies who'd just arrived. "Luke has gone after our suspect," he said. "Let's go give him some help."

The two men nodded and followed Ben as he ran in the direction that the kidnapper and Luke had gone. They were almost to the tree line of the forest when Luke stepped out into the field and jogged toward them.

He halted in front of them and wiped sweat from his forehead. "I lost him," he said. "There are a lot of trails that lead into the mountains hidden in those trees.

It was impossible to find one he might have taken. It was as if he just disappeared."

Ben stared at the forest for a moment before he nodded. "That doesn't surprise me. There's some rugged country in this area. If we want to catch this guy, I'd better get a search team out here." He pulled his shoulder mic toward his mouth and requested a canine search team at Wears Valley, informing dispatch that there was an escaped suspect in area.

"Ten-four, Unit 1. Will advise ETA as soon as possible."

Ben glanced back at the car, which was still smoking, and saw that the EMTs had brought a gurney to the scene and lifted Hannah onto it. He turned to Luke. "I'm turning the search party over to you so that I can go to the hospital with Hannah. Clara will radio back with the estimated time of arrival for the team. Keep me posted on what's happening."

Luke nodded. "I will." His gaze went to the EMTs who were preparing to push the gurney toward the ambulance and then back to Ben. "You go on and take care of Hannah. We'll make out fine here."

For a moment the awful thought of what might have happened to Hannah washed over Ben. If their suspect had chosen to turn onto another road before Ben and Luke got to him, he would have disappeared with Hannah. Thankfully they'd arrived in time, but there were still lots of unanswered questions.

What had prompted the man to abduct Hannah? Was she a random victim, or had there been a motive behind his actions? Random acts of violence were fairly rare—

attackers usually had a reason and a specific victim in mind when they chose to lash out. But could Hannah truly have been targeted? Ben couldn't believe that anybody would want to deliberately hurt her. Everyone in town knew her as a dedicated mother who had worked hard since the death of her husband to provide a good life for her daughter and herself.

Even those who didn't know her well knew of her larger-than-life husband who had charmed everyone in town when he'd married Hannah and moved there six years ago. In a community such as theirs where horses played an important role, Shane had been the celebrity in their midst as the World Mounted Archery League champion. He hadn't missed an opportunity to cash in on his fame and had been in demand for conducting clinics and judging competitions all over the world. That was, until one night in Houston when he was mugged and killed while returning to his hotel.

Now Hannah was raising their child alone, and had become one of the leading experts on mounted archery in the country. People came from all over the world to attend her training sessions. Today, all that had almost come to an end. The thought made Ben's stomach roil, and he hurried to catch up with the EMTs as they approached the ambulance. "Joe," he called out. The paramedic turned and stopped as Ben ran toward him. "How is she?"

"I can't find any broken bones, but you never can tell about internal injuries. We need to get that checked out and attend to the cut on her head. We'll know more when the doctor can run some tests at the hospital."

Ben glanced at the squad car he and Luke had arrived in and back to Joe. "Could I ride to the hospital with you? I need to leave my car here for Luke."

"Sure," Joe said.

Ben followed behind as the two EMTs pushed the gurney to the waiting ambulance and loaded Hannah inside. When Joe had Hannah settled and ready to be transported, Ben climbed in. Hannah looked up at him and smiled when he sat down next to her.

"Are you okay, Ben?" she asked.

The question surprised him. "Me? I'm fine. It's you we should be worried about. You're the one who's just been through a terrifying experience."

She reached out and clasped his hand. "I know you, Ben Whitman, and I know you care about every victim. You always put your whole self into righting every wrong you encounter, but it leaves you drained afterward. I'm afraid the stress of your job is going to get to you after a while, and I don't want that to happen. The people of this county need you, and I think I just realized today how much Faith and I need you, too. You're the best friend I've ever had."

He smiled and gave her hand a squeeze. "I'm glad you think of me that way—as someone you can count on. I always promised Shane that I would look after his girls while he was away, and I'll never break that promise. You can count on me."

She smiled and closed her eyes. After a moment he

realized she had drifted off to sleep. He glanced over his shoulder at Joe. "Is it okay for her to sleep?"

Joe nodded. "Yeah. We used to think that anyone with a head injury should be kept awake, but that theory has been proven untrue. Now doctors believe healing starts when the patient is asleep. She's hooked to a monitor that's checking her blood pressure and heart rate. So I'll let her rest until we get to the hospital."

Ben turned back to Hannah, but he didn't let go of her hand. He held it as he watched her sleep, all the way to the hospital.

TWO

Hannah opened her eyes, but she couldn't figure out where she was. She felt pressure on her hand and turned her head to see Ben sitting beside her with his hand wrapped around hers. A frown pulled at her forehead, and then the memory of what she'd endured returned.

Noticing her open eyes, Ben leaned forward and smiled. "We're at the hospital, Hannah. Joe is getting ready to take you into the emergency room, but I'll be in the waiting room while the doctor examines you."

She smiled and nodded. "Thanks, Ben. Would you do something for me?"

"Sure. What is it?"

"I had only intended to run a few errands before going home. Valerie is with Faith. She must be worried by this time. Will you call and let her know what happened and ask her to stay with Faith until I can get home?"

"Don't worry. I'll take care of it."

"We're ready to take you in, Hannah." Joe's voice from the back of the ambulance interrupted them. "Ben can come back to the exam room as soon as the doctor is through checking you out."

Hannah smiled up at Ben. "Then I'll see you later."

He nodded. "Later."

Ben looked as if he wanted to say more, but he turned and climbed from the ambulance. Joe and his partner pulled the gurney out, and she caught one last glimpse of Ben before they rolled her through the emergency bay of the hospital.

Inside they were met by a nurse who ushered them to an exam room. As soon as they had her situated in a bed, Joe gave the nurse the information about her vitals and the extent of her noticeable injuries, and then he disappeared into the hallway. The nurse leaned over the bed and smiled. "Hi, Hannah. My name is Cindy. The doctor will be with you in a moment. Are you feeling pain anywhere?"

Hannah touched the cut on her head that Joe had placed a temporary bandage on. "This cut on my head stings, but that's the worst of it."

Cindy examined the cut and nodded. "That doesn't look too bad, but I'm sure it stings. I'll get that cleaned up before the doctor sees you."

Hannah winced and bit down on her lip as the nurse began to wipe at the cut. The pain subsided as a cool ointment of some kind was spread across her forehead and then a gauze pad applied. Before either one of them could say anything, the door opened, and a middle-aged man wearing a white lab coat and a stethoscope around his neck walked into the room.

He stopped at the side of the bed and waited for the nurse to move out of the way before he smiled and stepped closer to her. "Hello, Mrs. Riley. I'm Doctor Denton. I hear you've had quite an experience this afternoon. Are you in pain anywhere?"

Hannah shook her head. "Nothing serious—just some soreness from cuts and bruises."

"That's good." He glanced at the monitors beside her bed and nodded before turning back to her. "Your vitals look good, but you do have the cut on your head. Let me look at it."

Hannah didn't move as he pulled the bandage back and examined the cut. "Is it very deep?"

He shook his head and pressed the gauze back in place. "No, it should heal very cleanly. Of course, we need to make sure there aren't any other injuries you haven't yet noticed. I've ordered a CT scan to determine if you have any internal injuries. As soon as I've looked at it, I'll be back to examine you further. Do you have any questions?"

"No. I did wonder, though, when I'll be able to see my friend."

"Sheriff Whitman? I talked with him in the waiting room. He's very anxious to find out if you're okay. I'll let him come back soon."

For the moment there was nothing else Hannah could do but accept the doctor's decision. If she'd had her way, Ben would have been with her every minute since she got to the hospital. He was the only person she'd been able to depend on since Shane died. He had been there the minute he heard and hadn't left her side during the days leading up to the funeral. Since then, he'd done everything he could for her and Faith whenever they needed him. She didn't know what she'd done to deserve a friend like Ben, but she was thankful for him.

Thirty minutes later, the tests were completed and Hannah was settled back in the bed in the emergency room as she waited for the doctor. He didn't keep her waiting long. When he walked in, he was smiling, which she took to be a good sign. He didn't waste time telling her what the results of the tests were.

"Well, Mrs. Riley, the CT scan shows no internal injuries. You're a very fortunate young lady to have survived a car crash like that with nothing worse to show for it than cuts and bruises."

"I know," Hannah said. "I'm very thankful. Everyone here has been extremely nice to me, but I hope you're going to let me go home now. I have a daughter I need to see about."

He nodded. "I know. Sheriff Whitman told me. I'm not going to keep you, but I suggest you take it easy for a few days. Come back to the emergency room if you have any problems, though."

"I will."

"Now, I'm going out to tell the sheriff he can come back to see you. The nurse will be in to discharge you."

"Thank you, Doctor," she said as he turned and walked from the room.

She lay back on the bed and waited for a few minutes, and then she heard Ben's footsteps in the hallway. She smiled at how she had come to recognize the sound his boots made as he walked. The doctor had left the door open, and Ben stopped before he entered and let his gaze rake over her.

He held the Stetson hat he always wore in his hands, and his fingers clutched the brim. He almost looked as if he was afraid to enter. She pushed up in bed and smiled. "Are you going to stand there, or are you coming in?"

The muscles in his throat constricted as he swallowed. Then, without taking his eyes off her, he walked over to her bed. "How are you feeling?" She smiled and reached for his hand. He wrapped his fingers around hers and held them tightly. "I've been going out of my mind in that waiting room," he admitted. "I was afraid you were hurt badly and they weren't telling me."

The rasp in his voice surprised her, and she let her gaze move over his face. She'd known Ben for years, but she'd never seen the look in his eyes that she saw now. It was so much more than just concern. It looked like he had just experienced agony, and her heart pricked. Had he really been that worried about her?

"Ben," she said as she squeezed his hand, "I'm okay. The doctor says there are no serious injuries. So quit worrying."

He released a long breath and closed his eyes for a moment. "Hannah, when that car went off the road, I knew if you died it would be my fault because it was my bullet that hit the tire. I don't think I could've lived with myself if I was the cause of you being killed."

She smiled and swung her legs over the side of the

bed. "I prefer to think that you saved my life. If it wasn't for you, that guy would have killed me." When she was standing in front of him, she put her arms around him and gave him a hug. "Thank you for being there again for me, Ben."

Slowly his arms encircled her, and he gave her a quick hug before he pulled back. "Anytime, Hannah. All you have to do is call."

She laughed. "That's good to know. Now could you do something else for me?"

"What?"

"Take me home. I'm ready to get out of this place."

He opened his mouth to speak, and then a look of horror flashed across his face. "I can't."

She stared at him and frowned. "Why not?"

"Because I left my car out at the crash scene for Luke, and yours is still smashed into that tree. We don't have a way to get either of us home."

She laughed and shook her head. "Did it not occur to you to drive your car and let Luke ride back with one of the other deputies?"

He grinned and shook his head. "All I was thinking about was getting you to the hospital, and I didn't want you out of my sight. So Joe let me ride in the ambulance."

She placed her hands on her hips and arched an eyebrow. "Well, what do we do now?"

Ben turned his mouth to his shoulder mic. "Officer needs a squad car at the hospital emergency-room door to transport a victim home."

The radio crackled, and the dispatcher's voice answered. "Ten-four. Escort on the way. By the way, how is Hannah?"

Ben grimaced. "Clara, this is an official channel. It's not for personal use. Over and out."

Hannah couldn't help but laugh. "You're going to have to give up on trying to make Clara more professional. From what my grandfather told me, she's always been the biggest gossip in these hills."

"I know," Ben grumbled. "But she doesn't need to be spreading gossip about you right now. We need to keep you out of the spotlight as much as possible until we catch this guy who kidnapped you. Until that time, I'm going to keep a closer check on you."

His words startled Hannah, and she gasped. "You think this might have been more than a random abduction?"

"I don't know, but until we find out one way or the other, you have to watch your back. I'll be there to help." He glanced at his watch. "Now let's go to the emergency-room entrance and wait for our ride."

Hannah nodded and walked from the room with Ben right behind her. For a moment there she'd felt relief and a sense of security that her ordeal was over. But Ben had just reminded her that it wasn't.

She frowned as she tried to remember the words of her kidnapper when she'd asked him why he was doing this. Her heart raced as she recalled what he'd said. *All you need to know is that it's payback time.*

Payback for what? She hadn't gotten a close look at his face, just his eyes. They hadn't seemed familiar in that moment, but now she knew she would recognize them anywhere as she would the sound of his voice.

If someone had a grudge against her, then Ben was right. Her kidnapper wouldn't give up after one failed attempt. He'd be back, and the next time she might not be rescued as she'd been today.

From now on, she needed to be on guard every minute of the day.

Ben and Hannah reached the entrance to the emergency-room door just as the squad car pulled into the parking lot. He recognized the vehicle right away. It was the car he and Luke had been in when he received the call about the kidnapping. He frowned and glanced at his watch. It had been only two hours since the car crash. If Luke was back, that meant the search around the crash site was over. Why were they done so soon? Did they have the suspect in custody?

Luke pulled to a stop at the door, and Ben and Hannah stepped outside. As they approached the car, the passenger-side window rolled down. Ben leaned over to peer inside. Before he could speak, he noticed another vehicle driving into the parking lot. It was his truck.

"What's going on, Luke?" he asked. "Why aren't you out at the crime scene?"

Luke exhaled and shook his head. "The dogs lost the scent at a road on the other side of the woods. The handlers tried to find it again, but it looked hopeless. We figured he must have had a car waiting there."

Ben didn't like the sound of that. If the suspect had a car parked, or a getaway driver waiting, then Hannah's abduction had been planned in advance. Perhaps the plan had been to drive onto a mountain trail and kill her before escaping in another car that the police wouldn't be looking for. Chills raced down his spine at how easily that could have happened if things had gone just a little differently.

"So they've given up the search?"

Luke shook his head. "No. We may not be able to catch the guy tonight, but there's still a chance he left some evidence behind—something we can use to track him down. I came into town to get some more equipment for the search. I happened to be at the station when you called in. I'd already told Andy Walker to go back with me to join in the search, so I thought we could drop your truck off here, and he could ride out there with me."

Ben glanced at the newest deputy on the force as Andy climbed from his truck and walked toward him. "Evening, Sheriff," he said as he came to a stop beside him. "I left your truck running."

Ben nodded. "Thanks, Andy." He turned his attention back to Luke. "I'll see that Hannah gets home safely, and then I'll join you out there."

"Take your time, Sheriff. We've got it under control," Luke said as Andy got into the car.

They waved as they drove out of the parking lot. Ben turned to Hannah and took her by the arm. "Let's get you home."

She smiled. "Thanks, Ben. I'm beginning to feel tired."

He helped her into the truck before he walked around and got in on the driver's side. Out of the corner of his eye he saw her lay her head back on the headrest and close her eyes. He turned his head and stared at her for a moment.

He remembered the first time he'd seen her. He'd stopped by her grandfather's ranch to check on him that day, and she'd arrived just after he'd gotten there. She was fresh out of college and excited about her future. He could still remember the blue sundress she'd been wearing and how her eyes lit up when she caught sight of her grandfather. She'd run to him and thrown herself into his arms.

Ben had stood there, watching the reunion, unable to move. He didn't think he'd ever seen a more beautiful woman, and for a minute he couldn't speak. Then she'd turned to him, her dimple winking at him, and smiled. "You must be Ben Whitman. Grandfather has told me so much about you. I know we're going to be great friends."

She'd been right. Over the years they'd grown close. He'd been there for her when she lost her grandfather, and then again when she'd lost her husband. He'd loved her daughter as if she were his own. But she'd been there for him, too. When his mother passed away unexpectedly not long after Hannah was widowed, she had put aside her own grief to be by his side. Her positive attitude and encouragement had helped pull him through those dark times. The thought that he might have lost her in his life today hit like a punch to the stomach every time he thought about it.

As they approached the turnoff to Tumbling Creek

Ranch, she roused, blinked and sat up. "Oh, we're almost home. I'm sorry I wasn't better company on the ride."

"No problem," he said. "I wish I could come in and see Faith, but I need to get out to Wears Valley and see if the search team has found anything. I'll check in with you tomorrow to see how you're feeling."

"I'm sure I'll be fine, but you know it's always good to hear from you."

"You be sure and follow the doctor's orders. You know he wants you to get all the rest you can. So take it easy for a few days. You have Valerie to take care of Faith, and you can turn the horses over to Dusty."

She nodded. "I'm going to try. It's good that I have backup I can count on. Valerie's only been with us a few weeks, but she's doing a great job as Faith's nanny. As for Dusty, he was with Grandfather before I came, and he knows how this ranch is run. I was fortunate to have him after I lost my grandfather."

"Yeah. Then he really took on more responsibilities when Shane died."

He sensed, rather than saw, her posture stiffen. "I guess you could say that."

There was a harshness in her tone that he'd never heard before, and he could tell it had something to do with Shane. She must be exhausted—when she was at full strength, she usually kept a tight lid on her emotions whenever she talked about Shane. He'd always assumed that was because it was too painful for her to remember him. The fact that he'd been murdered in Houston one night after teaching a clinic had been a shock to all of them, and he didn't think she'd ever recovered.

He cut his eyes toward her. "I hope I haven't brought up some painful memories for you. I don't want to cause you to go back to that place you were in right after Shane's death."

She sighed. "I don't want to go back there, either. I guess everything that happened today brought it all back to me. When I thought that man was going to kill me, all I could think of was how Faith was going to suffer. She's already lost her father. If I'd been killed, she would have had to grow up without a mother, too."

"But the important thing is that you didn't die. You're still here for her. You need to focus on being thankful for that."

She turned her head away and stared out the window. "Don't pay attention to me. I'm still shaken from what happened earlier. I shouldn't have said anything."

The tone of her voice told him that there was something else bothering her. When she didn't explain further, he was tempted to ask more about what she'd just said. However, her silence made it evident she didn't want to discuss it. After the ordeal she'd already been through, he didn't want to upset her any further. He directed his attention back to the road and didn't say anything else.

Within a few minutes, they had arrived at Hannah's house, and he pulled to a stop in the circle driveway. He switched off the engine and turned to face her. "Well, here we are. Do you want me to see you to the door?"

She shook her head. "Valerie is here. She'll get Faith ready for bed, and then I'm going to try to get a good night's sleep." She hesitated for a moment and then placed her hand on his arm. "Thank you again for rescuing me today, Ben."

He swallowed and stared into her eyes. "Hannah, I hope you know I'll always be there for you."

She smiled. "I know you will, but I'm afraid I've relied on you too much since Shane died. Sometimes I think you put your life on hold just to help me out."

"You would do the same for me. That's what friends do."

She nodded. "I know, but it's time for me to stand on my own two feet."

"What do you mean?"

She stared out the windshield for a few moments before she turned back to face him. "I had a lot of time to think after I got to the hospital, and I made some decisions."

Her tone of voice alarmed Ben, and he frowned. "Decisions about what?"

"There are things that I've wanted to do but held off because I didn't have the courage to tackle them. Shane's celebrity in the sport of mounted archery has cast a shadow over everything I've achieved for myself. I was competing when I met Shane, but after we were married, he discouraged me from continuing. He said I wasn't good enough to really make it to the top. Every time I brought it up, he would rattle off all my weaknesses that made me an unlikely competitor. He made me doubt my ability, and I gave up the idea I'd ever compete again."

"I'm sorry, Hannah. I never knew that."

She shrugged. "Well, it's not something you talk about. In my heart I knew I was a good rider and an excellent archer, but Shane's criticisms made me doubt myself so that I became afraid to enter competitions. That all changed when I thought I was going to die. A few weeks ago I was invited to participate in the World Horseback Archery League's competition, but I'd decided I wouldn't go. Now I've changed my mind. I'm going to do it. I can't live in the past. From now on, I'm going to make a good life for Faith and me because we're all the family that either of us has."

"Good for you. I'm glad you've decided to return to competing. Where is the competition being held?"

"Korea."

He didn't expect to be stunned by her answer, but he was. "Korea?"

She nodded. "Yes."

He gave his head a slight shake and frowned. "Why didn't you tell me about this?"

"Because I didn't think I would go, but now I am."

"But…but… Korea," he stammered. "That's a long way from home."

She smiled, reached over and patted him on the hand. "Don't worry. We won't be gone long. As soon as the competition is over, we'll come back."

"You're saying we, so I guess you're taking Faith with you."

"I am. I'll talk to her teacher, and we'll work something out. She's only four and in kindergarten. It's not like I have to worry about her missing tests or important homework. It will be good for her to see a different culture, and it will give us a chance to spend some time together. Don't worry. We won't be gone long."

He swallowed the sick feeling he had at the thought of Hannah and Faith being away from him and nodded. "Okay. If that's what you want. I'll do anything I can to help you finish training and prepare for your trip before you leave."

She smiled. "I appreciate that Ben. I have a lot to do before I leave. There are passports to get and travel to plan. And I need to find out if we need special visas or vaccinations, but I think this trip is going to be good for us. It will give me a chance to reevaluate my life and see what I want to do in the future."

Having said that, she climbed from the truck and slowly made her way up the steps to the front porch. Ben sat in his truck for a moment as he thought about the things Hannah had said. He'd sensed a new determination in her tonight that hadn't been there in a very long time. She wanted a new life for herself and her daughter. If that's what she wanted, he was going to do everything he could to make it happen. He'd been doing that for years, and he'd keep on as long as he had breath in his body.

Before she could get on with her life, however, there was still the question of why she'd been kidnapped today. If she and Faith were to have a secure future, he had to find out who had a reason to hurt her. From the things she'd hinted at but left unsaid tonight, he realized that there might be a lot of secrets in the past that could hold the answers. If there were, he intended to find the answers.

THREE

Faith came running to meet her the minute Hannah walked in the door. Her blond ponytail swung back and forth as she hurled herself at her mother. "Mommy! I thought you'd never get home."

Hannah caught the child and swung her up in her arms. For a minute she stood there with her arms wrapped around her daughter with her eyes closed and said a prayer of thanks for coming home safely. This day could have had an entirely different ending.

Faith straightened in her mother's arms and was about to say something when her eyes opened in alarm as she stared at the bandage on Hannah's head. "What's wrong with your head, Mommy?"

A feeble smile pulled at Hannah's lips. "It's nothing, darling. I just cut my head, but it's all right. Ben took me to the hospital, and the doctor fixed it. He said I was fine."

Faith tilted her head to one side and continued to stare at the bandage. "Does it hurt?"

"Not anymore," she said as she stared into Faith's

blue eyes. "But enough about me. How was school today?"

Faith looked at the bandage once more before she smiled and patted her mother's cheek. "It was a good day. It's still my turn to be the teacher's helper. It made Janie Culver jealous because I got to do more than she did when it was her turn."

"Well, did you remind Janie that her turn will come back around when Miss Morris draws her name again?"

Faith nodded. "I did, but she still wouldn't play with me."

Hannah kissed Faith on the cheek and set her down so that she was standing in front of her. "What do we always say when someone's not nice to us?"

Faith tilted her head to one side and put her finger up to her chin, looking as serious as it was possible for an adorable four-year-old to look. "We treat them like they're a friend and keep on being nice to them."

"That's right," Hannah said as she glanced up and saw Valerie coming into the entry where they stood. Although she'd been with them only a few weeks, Hannah had come to depend on her.

Over the past year, her classes in mounted archery had increased to the point that she'd often found herself in need of someone to help out with Faith. Her ad in the local newspaper had attracted several applicants for the job of Faith's nanny, but none of them had impressed her like Valerie had. From the first day she'd fit in like she'd always been at their ranch, and Hannah had found herself depending more and more on her assistance.

Valerie held a dish towel, and she wiped her hands on it as Hannah came to a stop. A frown puckered her forehead as her gaze quickly scanned Hannah's face. "How are you feeling?"

Hannah glanced down at Faith, frowned and shook her head. She didn't want to discuss what had happened earlier in front of Faith. "I'm fine," she answered. "What's that wonderful smell?"

Faith grinned as if she had a big secret. "Maria had to leave early, so I helped Valerie make spaghetti, and it's good."

Hannah frowned. Maria, the cook who had begun work at the ranch years ago when her grandparents were alive, hadn't said anything to her about needing to take off early.

"Why did Maria have to leave?"

"Her sister called and said she was sick. Maria wanted to go check on her, and I told her not to worry. Faith and I could make dinner tonight," Valerie said.

Hannah started to make a comment about the sister who seemed to always suffer from some ache or pain. Instead she let her mouth drop open and bent over so that she was staring into her child's eyes. "You helped Valerie make dinner? Then it must really be good."

Faith's chest puffed out with pride. "We saved you some."

Hannah closed her eyes and smacked her lips as if she was getting ready to devour a feast fit for a king. "I can hardly wait."

Valerie smiled and started to turn back toward the kitchen. "I'll warm up your plate. You must be starved."

Hannah reached out and stopped her before Valerie could leave the room. "I can get it. I know you're in a hurry to get home. I've kept you later than usual."

Valerie cast a quick glance at Faith before she replied. "I don't mind. Anytime you need me, I'm glad to help out. I'd rather be here with you two than watching TV alone in my apartment."

Hannah studied the young woman for a moment. Valerie Patrick was only a few years younger than Hannah, but something about her made her seem much older. Perhaps it was the way her eyes appeared to fill with sadness sometimes when she looked at Faith. Hannah had never questioned Valerie about her past, but she had confided in her before she'd come to work at the ranch that she'd had a miscarriage several years ago when her husband died unexpectedly. She had come to the Smokies in hopes of starting a new life and was grateful to Hannah for giving her the opportunity to make a living doing something she enjoyed.

Sometimes, though, Hannah thought she asked too much of Valerie. She had taken on more and more responsibilities since coming here, and Hannah felt guilty about taking up so much of her time. "I keep telling you to get out more. Maybe if you'd go to church with us Sunday, you could meet someone near your age."

Valerie seemed to consider it for a moment before she smiled. "I think I'd like that. Let me know what time you're leaving, and I'll be here to go with you." She reached for Faith's hand. "But for now, why don't I go help Faith through her bath and get her ready for bed while you eat? Then you can come up and tuck her in for the night."

Suddenly Hannah felt so tired. It had been a long day. She was exhausted and hungry, and that spaghetti smelled really good. "Thanks, Valerie. Go on upstairs with Faith, and I'll be up in a few minutes."

Hannah watched as her daughter grabbed Valerie's hand and dragged her toward the stairway. Her eyes sparkled, and she giggled in her little girl way as they climbed toward the upstairs. "Can I have some bubble bath tonight?"

Her excited voice made Hannah smile. She heard Valerie's muffled agreement as they disappeared down the second-floor hallway. Smiling, Hannah walked into the kitchen. A plate covered in aluminum foil sat on the table.

She removed the foil, placed the plate in the microwave and within minutes was sitting at the kitchen table practically inhaling the food. She hadn't eaten much lunch, and now she realized how hungry she was. The thought of Faith telling her how she'd helped cook the spaghetti flashed in Hannah's mind, and she suddenly put her fork down and covered her face with her hands.

For a moment she let the tears flow as she thought about how differently things could have been tonight if she'd been killed. Thankfully, Ben and Luke had come to her rescue.

Ben's warning echoed in her mind again, and she swallowed the fear that rose in her throat. If someone had a grudge against her, it had to have something to do with Shane. Ben and everybody else in town thought of him as the bigger-than-life local hero. If only they knew what she'd endured, they would be shocked at the real Shane Riley she'd come to know. But to reveal the ugly truth would only make their family the target of public gossip and ridicule. That would hurt Faith in particular, who didn't remember her father and who believed in all the stories she'd heard of what a good man he'd been.

Even after all these years, Hannah couldn't figure out how she could have been so naive to fall for such a con man. Mounted archery competition was an expensive sport. Most competitions, even international ones, required high entrance fees as well as travel and transportation for a horse, and the prize most of the time was a trophy or medal, not money like rodeo competitions. His fees for the workshops he conducted didn't start to cover the expenses of the sport.

Shane had played the loving and attentive boyfriend until they were married and he gained access to the money the ranch brought in. At first she'd been happy to help him until she discovered that most of the money was spent on his extravagant lifestyle and the women he met while competing and teaching workshops.

Even after she found out about the women, she'd held out hope he would settle down when she became pregnant, but he'd been furious at any attempt she'd made to curtail his activities. By the time he was killed, their marriage had been over for several years but she had hung on to it in public to save face. Sometimes she wondered how she'd been able to do it.

The whole experience had taught her a lesson, though. She didn't intend to fall in love again. She'd seen how a man could pretend to be one thing and be entirely different. She didn't intend to go down that path again.

"Faith's in bed and waiting for you to come up."

Valerie's voice jerked her from her thoughts, and Hannah looked up to see her standing in the door. "Thanks for getting her ready. Now you go on home, and don't worry about coming to get Faith ready for school tomorrow. I'll tell Dusty to take care of the morning chores, and I'll drop her off myself. But I'd like for you to pick her up from school as usual."

Valerie looked as if she was about to object but then changed her mind. "If you're sure you don't need me to take her to school, it would help me out. I have some errands I could take care of in the morning."

Hannah pushed up from the table. "I don't plan on getting out or doing much tomorrow, so I'll see you tomorrow afternoon."

Valerie smiled and turned toward the front door. Hannah followed her and watched until she had pulled away from the house. Then she locked the front door and climbed the stairs to Faith's room.

She was already in bed, propped up on two pillows, and held the book they'd been reading. "Mommy, read me some more."

Hannah smiled and snuggled up in the bed with her daughter. They'd read only a few pages when Faith yawned, and Hannah set the book down. "You're getting sleepy," she said. "Why don't you say your prayers, and I'll tuck you in."

Faith nodded, laced her fingers together and held them under her chin. Then she closed her eyes and bowed her head. "God bless Mommy, and Valerie, and Dusty, and Ben, and Miss Morris. And God bless Janie Culver and help her to be my friend again. Amen."

Hannah reached for the covers to tuck Faith in, but she suddenly closed her eyes again and prayed the ending that she'd been adding for the past few weeks. "And please make Mommy let me get a new puppy."

With a grin on her face, she opened her eyes and burrowed down into the covers. Hannah laughed as she leaned over and kissed her daughter good-night. "Sweet dreams, baby girl. I love you."

"I love you, too, Mommy."

Hannah walked to the door and turned out the light. The Winnie the Pooh night-light that they always left on cast a glow across the bed. Hannah smiled once more before she slipped from the room and headed back downstairs.

Once in the kitchen, she poured herself a cup of coffee and sat at the table drinking it as she thought of how thankful she was for her child. When the cup was drained, she set it in the sink and walked to the back door.

She locked it and then flipped off the overhead lights. Only the hall light filtered into the kitchen as she stared out the door toward the barn. She was about to turn away when movement in the shadows caught her eye.

She stood still as if she were frozen and watched as a figure emerged from beside the barn and eased toward the house. In the dark she couldn't make out any features, but from what she could see of the height and build, it had to be a man.

He crept closer until he was about halfway between the barn and the house. He stopped and stood still as he faced toward her. She knew he couldn't see her standing in the darkened kitchen, but she couldn't stop the chills that ran down her spine.

After a few minutes, he turned back toward the barn and melted into the shadows. She stayed there watching for the next ten minutes, but he never reappeared. Could that have been the man who kidnapped her earlier? If so, what did he gain by spying on her house?

She bit down on her lip and tried to calm her shaking body. Maybe it really was time to get a dog, one that could alert them when someone came around— and a security system, too. She'd check on that first thing tomorrow.

For now, though, she had to get through this night, and something told her sleeping was going to be difficult. She slipped from the room and into the den where her grandfather had built a wall safe. Her shaking fingers misdialed the combination twice before the door finally opened.

She reached inside and pulled out her grandfather's handgun and the clips of ammunition he'd always kept there. Then she closed the safe, and clutching the gun to her chest, she sank down on the couch.

Reason told her that the man who'd been spying on

her house would have broken in then if he'd meant to, but she couldn't take a chance that he might return to try to harm her or her daughter. She had a gun. It was loaded, and she was ready if trouble came.

It was going to be a long night.

At six o'clock the next morning, Ben pulled into the driveway at Little Pigeon Ranch, the dude ranch owned and operated by his best friend, Dean Harwell. He headed for the barn, knowing Dean had probably been up for an hour and was getting ready for another busy day. When Ben pulled to a stop, he saw his friend leading a horse out of the barn.

Dean threw up his hand in welcome when he caught sight of Ben's truck coming down the driveway. Grinning, he stopped and waited while Ben climbed out of the vehicle. "You're out kind of early, aren't you? I thought you told me yesterday you were going to take a few hours off today and do some trout fishing. Did you change your mind?"

"I had everything arranged for Luke to fill in for me today, but we had some excitement yesterday afternoon."

Dean pulled on the lead attached to the horse's halter and started toward the corral. "Let me put this horse up, and you can tell me all about it."

"That's why I came by," Ben called out as Dean walked away.

As Ben waited for Dean to return, a slight smile pulled at his lips. He knew this ranch almost as well as he knew his own. He'd become friends with Dean soon after Dean had come to live with his grandparents when they were both still kids. They'd been inseparable through school as they explored the trails in the mountains they both loved. By the time they graduated from high school, they'd become valuable members of the search and rescue teams that helped find missing persons in the vast wilderness of the Smokies. Then they'd drifted apart when they had gone to separate colleges.

He had moved back home while still in his midtwenties, and Dean had arrived back at his grandparents' home a few years later. They'd both returned to the mountains they loved, and each had brought his own baggage with him. Maybe that's why it was so easy for them to resume their friendship after not seeing each other for years. They needed the support of each other as they battled the addictions and overcame the grief that had driven their lives for too many years.

They'd hung in there, though, and had been there for each other during the darkest time of their lives. Their struggles had paid off. Now Little Pigeon Ranch was not just a prosperous business, but a happy home for Dean, his wife, Gwen, and their daughter, Maggie.

Ben still couldn't believe at times that he was the sheriff in the community where he'd grown up. But most of all he often thought of how he and Dean had struggled to get where they were today. He knew their achievements wouldn't have been possible if they hadn't shared a deep faith in God that guided them to the lives they had today.

"Now tell me what happened yesterday."

Ben jerked around and frowned as Dean stepped up

beside him. "Sorry about that," he said. "I was lost in thought and didn't hear you."

Dean chuckled. "You must have really had a bad day yesterday. What happened?"

Ben pulled the hat from his head and rubbed the back of his neck. "The day had been fairly routine until I got the message that Hannah had been abducted from Bart's Stop and Shop."

Dean's eyes rounded like saucers. "Hannah Riley? Your Hannah Riley?"

Ben frowned and pushed his hat back down on his head. "Yes, Hannah Riley, but she's not *my* Hannah Riley," he growled.

Dean tried to smother the grin that pulled at his lips, but he wasn't successful. Ben straightened his shoulders and glared at him. Why did Dean always act like this whenever Hannah's name was mentioned? Ben had explained to him over and over that he and Hannah were just friends, but Dean always appeared to read more into the relationship than what it really was.

Dean waved his hand in dismissal, but his grin didn't disappear. "Whatever you say. Now tell me what happened."

As quickly as he could, Ben gave Dean all the details of the abduction yesterday, Hannah's trip to the hospital and the search that hadn't turned up any clues to the identity of the suspect.

"The good thing," Ben said, "is that Hannah wasn't seriously injured, and she's safe back at home."

Dean rubbed his chin and frowned as he mulled over what Ben had just told him. Dean had been a big-city detective for a number of years, and when it came to tracking down criminals, Ben trusted his instincts without reservations. "Do you think this was random or maybe planned?"

Ben shrugged. "I don't know, but I'm leaning toward the idea that it was planned. His escape was planned in advance, with a car waiting for him. This wasn't just a crime of opportunity. Besides, the guy told her at one point that it was for payback."

"Payback?"

"Yeah. She had no idea what that meant. She couldn't think of anyone that she'd had a disagreement with."

Dean was silent for a moment before he spoke. "Do you think it could have anything to do with her dead husband? He probably had a lot of people who were jealous because of his success."

Ben nodded. "That thought crossed my mind, but there's no way of knowing at this point. For the time being I'm going to keep an eye on her just in case this guy has something else planned. I don't intend for anything to happen to Hannah or Faith if I can help it."

Dean's eyebrows arched, and his grin grew larger. "And she's just a friend, huh? It sounds like she might be more than that."

Ben shook his head and scowled at Dean. "Cut it out. You know I'm not going to ever go there with another woman. I learned my lesson a long time ago."

Dean sighed. "Ben, when I came back here, I didn't think there was a chance that Gwen and I would ever get back together. My police work had me so messed up that I was a danger to her—she was right to walk out on me. And even after I left that all behind and came back here, I knew I had a long way to go before I could be the man she fell in love with again… If she was even willing to ever give me another chance. But you kept after me and encouraged me, and look where we are today. We're married again, we have a daughter and are happier than I could ever imagine being. I want the same for you."

As it did every time Dean brought up the past, Ben's heart constricted, and pictures of a long-ago night filled his head. "The difference is that you didn't kill Gwen like I did Laura."

"You didn't kill Laura," Dean said. "She was driving the car that ran off the road and hit a tree."

Ben's eyes watered as they did every time he thought of Laura, the vivacious blonde who had stolen his heart in college. "But she wouldn't have been driving in that awful storm if I hadn't been so wasted. She kept begging me to leave that party, but I thought I was having too good a time drinking and smoking pot with my friends. When she finally convinced me to leave, I was in no condition to drive, and the storm that hadn't been so bad an hour before made the roads downright treacherous. I failed her that night. I lived, and she died. I can't forget that."

Dean took a step closer to him. "I've told you over and over that we both have things in our pasts that we'd like to change, but we can't. That doesn't mean we have to let them ruin our lives. It's time you forgave yourself. I want to see you as happy as Gwen and I are, but only you can decide to take that step."

Ben shook his head. "I will never take a chance on hurting another woman. I worry all the time that something will happen that will send me spiraling back to where I was then. I can't take a chance on hurting another woman, and especially one as wonderful as Hannah."

"Then all I know to do for you is to pray. I want you to find happiness. You deserve it. If it wasn't for you, I would never have kicked my addiction."

Ben reached out and bumped Dean's shoulder with his fist. "Thanks, buddy, but you give me more credit than I deserve. You'd already made the decision to turn your life around by the time you left the force and moved back here." He glanced down at his watch and frowned. "I didn't realize it was getting so late. I need to run by Hannah's house and see how she's doing this morning. Then I think I'll grab a few hours of sleep before I go to the station. I'll talk to you later."

Dean nodded. "Later," he said as he slipped his hands in the pockets of his jeans. Ben was almost back to his car before Dean called out to him. "And tell Hannah that I'm glad she wasn't hurt yesterday. Gwen and I'll go over later today and check on her."

"Thanks," Ben called as he waved over his shoulder.

"And while you're at it—" Dean's raised voice caused Ben to stop in his tracks "—if you really want to cheer her up after her ordeal, why don't you ask her out to dinner?"

"You know we go out to dinner all the time," Ben called back.

"Yeah, but you always have Faith with you. No one can relax with a four-year-old tagging along. Why not try doing something just the two of you?"

Ben opened the door to his truck and glared back at his friend. "And I think you're trying again to push me into dating, which I've told you I don't intend to do. See you later."

He jumped in the truck before Dean had a chance to respond and pulled onto the road that led back into town. Hannah's ranch was only a few miles off this road, and he did want to see her before he went home. Because she was his friend, the granddaughter of a man he'd greatly admired and the widow of a man who'd been his friend. Nothing else. That's all it was.

All he had to do was keep telling himself that.

FOUR

Hannah didn't know where she was when she first woke. The memory of sitting on the couch in an attempt to stay awake hit her, and she bolted upright. She remembered hearing the grandfather clock in the hallway strike two o'clock, but she couldn't recall anything after that—except for scattered fragments of dreams.

Her sleep had been plagued with visions of a man holding a gun on her playing over and over, and this morning she ached all over. The pain was probably a combination of the wreck yesterday and her restless night.

She pushed into a sitting position on the couch and yawned as the clock struck six. Her stomach growled, and she rose from the couch and stretched her arms over her head to ease her aching body before she headed to the kitchen.

She stopped at the doorway that led into the room and stared at Maria, the woman who, along with her husband, Dusty, had started to work for Hannah's grandfather before she was even born. In the beginning Maria had cooked in the bunkhouse kitchen for the hired men who worked on the ranch. Gradually, over the years the bunkhouse had been deserted as new employees chose marriage and family along with homes of their own.

When Hannah's grandmother died, Maria had become the cook and housekeeper for her grandfather. Now, years later, she and Dusty still lived in the house on the ranch that they'd lived in for years, and she still worked in the main house cooking and cleaning for Hannah and Faith.

Hannah didn't say anything for a moment but just watched the woman who stood at the stove cooking bacon and humming as her ample hips moved in time with the song drifting from the small kitchen radio.

"When did you get back?"

Maria said over her shoulder. "A little while ago. My sister was feeling better this morning. I may go back later to check on her." She turned to face Hannah, and her eyes widened in concern as she caught sight of the bandage on Hannah's head. "What happened to your head?"

Hannah stumbled farther into the kitchen, walked over to the cabinet and pulled out a cup. Then she picked up the coffeepot and poured a cup, sat down at the table and took a sip of the hot coffee. "I had an accident yesterday, and I guess I was still too keyed up to settle down."

Maria pushed the skillet off the stove eye, walked over to the table and stared down at Hannah, a worried expression on her face. "What kind of accident?"

Hannah took a deep breath and bit down on her lip before she responded. "A man abducted me at gunpoint while I was getting gas."

"Abducted you?" Maria exclaimed. Her gaze drifted over Hannah's face as if looking for more injuries. "Are you all right?"

Hannah nodded. "Yes, just still a little shaken up."

Maria reached across and grabbed Hannah's hand. "Tell me the whole story. What happened?"

For the next few minutes she related the events that had taken place the day before. When she'd finished, Maria closed her eyes and shuddered. "Oh, Hannah, you could have been killed."

"I know, but I'm okay. Just still shaken up a bit." She glanced over her shoulder to make sure that Faith hadn't come downstairs while she was talking. "Don't say anything about this in front of Faith. I don't want her to worry about me."

Maria's eyes darkened. "I won't. But Faith is a smart little girl. She's going to sense something is wrong."

"I know. I guess I'll just deal with her questions as they arise."

She'd no sooner finished speaking than Faith ran into the kitchen, her eyes bright and a smile on her face. She ran straight to her mother, jumped up in her lap and planted a big kiss on her cheek. "Morning, Mommy."

"Morning, Sugar Bear," Hannah said as she planted a kiss on Faith's soft cheek. "You look like you're ready for a big day."

Faith sighed. "I am, but I wish I could stay home with you."

The fear that Hannah had felt yesterday when she thought she was going to die and leave Faith an orphan swept over her, and she hugged her daughter tighter. The possibility of Faith being left alone or worse still being hurt made Hannah shudder. She couldn't get that man's words about her abduction being payback time out of her head. If the man knew where Faith went to school, the little girl might be targeted. Suddenly she didn't want her child out of her sight, and she tightened her arms around Faith's small body.

"Even if it's not a special day, I think we might make an exception for one time. How would you like to stay home with me today?"

Faith's eyes grew large. "Really? You'd let me do that?"

Hannah laughed. "We could spend the day together. You could help me with the horses, and you could practice your archery skills."

The excitement that had brightened Faith's eyes vanished as if a sudden thought had popped into her head. "I forgot. This is my last day to be the teacher's helper. If I'm not there, she'll let somebody else have my turn."

"But we could have so much fun," Hannah said. "I'll even let you—"

Her words were interrupted by a knock at the back door. Maria hurriedly wiped her hands on her apron and turned toward the door. "I'll get it." Hannah watched as Maria walked into the utility room at the back of the kitchen, and then the door creaked open. "Sheriff Whitman!" she heard Maria say.

The sound of heavy boots pounded against the floor

as Ben, holding his hat, walked into the kitchen. The minute Faith saw him she jumped out of Hannah's lap, gave a squeal of pleasure and raced toward him. Ben laughed as he bent over and scooped her up into his arms.

Ben's face beamed as he looked down at Faith. "How's my girl this morning?"

Faith threw her arms around his neck and hugged him. "I'm good. Why did you come to see us so early?"

Ben glanced past Faith to Hannah, and his gaze darkened. "I was passing by and thought I'd check on my two favorite girls and tell you that the new Disney movie is showing at the theater tonight. I thought if your mom is okay with it, I could take the two of you to see it."

Faith twisted in Ben's arms so that she faced her mother. "Can we, Mommy? Can we go with Ben to the movie tonight?"

Indecision warred in Hannah. Faith had been eagerly waiting for the movie to come to their theater, but it might be too dangerous. She frowned and hesitated before speaking.

"I don't know, honey. This is a weeknight, and you might be late getting to bed."

Faith tilted her head to one side and pursed her lips. "Maybe I could stay home from school tomorrow instead of today."

Ben's head jerked around, and he stared at Faith. "You're staying home today? What's wrong? Are you sick?"

Faith shook her head. "No, Mommy wanted us to

have a day together. I wanted to stay home, but today is my last day to be the teacher's helper. If I miss school, she'll choose somebody else. So if I could stay home tomorrow, I wouldn't miss my turn."

Ben's brows knit on his forehead, and he stared at Hannah. "You wanted Faith to stay home from school?"

Hannah lifted her chin and returned the questioning look he directed at her. "I thought it might be best."

Ben didn't say anything for a moment, but Hannah could sense his disapproval. Maria must have felt it, too, because she reached for Faith and pulled her out of Ben's arms. "Well, whatever you're going to do today, you need your breakfast. Sit down, and I'll get it for you."

Ben nodded. "That's a good idea, Maria. And while you're feeding Faith, Hannah and I will have a little talk in the den." He swept his arm toward the door to signal Hannah to proceed him. "This won't take but a minute."

Not looking forward to the lecture she expected to receive, Hannah reluctantly led Ben into the den. Once inside, he closed the door and turned to face her.

She spoke before he could. "I know what you're going to say, Ben. You think I'm overreacting to what happened yesterday, but I can't help it. That man said that he was abducting me for payback. What if I send her off to school, and he decides to take Faith since he didn't get me?" The fear that had been festering in her heart burst out, and she began to cry. "I'm scared something will happen to her, Ben."

He didn't say anything for a moment, just looked

at her as the muscle in his jaw flexed. Then he let out a long breath and reached for her. His arms circled her and drew her in so that her head rested against his chest. For a moment all she wanted was to feel safe, and she did with Ben.

"I understand," he whispered. "You had a horrible experience yesterday, and it's left you shaken. But you can't let this guy stop you from living your life. You need to go on as best you can. That means doing your work around the ranch and teaching your mounted archery classes. And Faith needs to go to school. Her teacher and principal aren't going to let anyone take her from there. If you're worried about her safety on the trip to and from school, I can take her myself today."

She knew he was right, but it did little to ease the worry she felt. She burrowed deeper against his chest. "Oh, Ben, what did we ever do to deserve a friend like you?"

He put his finger under her chin and raised her head so that he could stare down at her. A small smile pulled at his lips. "That works both ways, Hannah. I don't know why you'd settle for a friend like me when you deserve nothing but the best."

Hannah stepped back and regarded Ben with a troubled stare. "You've often hinted that there are some things in your background that I don't know about. I hope you know there's not anything that you can't tell me." She swallowed before she continued. "We all have secrets that we guard carefully, Ben."

"I know," he said, "but I don't want my past to touch you or Faith. The two of you are too important to me."

"As you are to us."

He cleared his throat. "Hannah, I want you to know that I will do everything I can to catch this guy, and I will protect you and Faith with my life."

His words warmed her heart, and a peaceful feeling surged through her. "You don't have to tell me that, Ben. You've always been there for me, and I appreciate it even if I do feel guilty about it sometimes."

"Why would you feel guilty?"

"Because I don't want you to spend your life worrying about Faith and me. You need to focus on yourself more—find someone and settle down."

A small laugh rippled from his mouth. "Well, I'm not looking, but if you find somebody you think is right for me, let me know. Now what do you say? Are you ready to get Faith off to school?"

She stared at him a moment before she looped her arm through his. "Thank you, Ben."

His eyebrows arched. "For what?"

"For always knowing the right thing to say. Let's go see if she's finished with her breakfast."

She led Ben back to the kitchen as she thought about what he'd said. Yesterday, a man had pointed a gun at her, and she was sure he wasn't done trying to hurt her. But Ben was right. She couldn't let the worry of that incident take over her life. She had a ranch to run and a daughter to raise.

It had seemed like a formidable task right after Shane had died, and she hadn't been sure she could do it. But Ben had been there supporting her and offering his help to her and Faith. She didn't think she could have done it without him.

Now he had promised to protect them, and she knew he would stop at nothing to see that no harm came to them. She had no idea what she would do without Ben in her life, and she hoped she never had to find out.

Faith's fingers were swallowed up in his hand as she and Ben walked down the hallway at the elementary school toward her classroom. Mrs. Mason, the principal, stood just outside the entrance to the library and observed all the students scurrying about in the building. She smiled when she saw Ben approach clutching Faith's hand.

"Good morning, Sheriff Whitman," she said with a smile and then looked down at Faith. "Aren't you fortunate to have the sheriff escorting you to class this morning?"

Faith nodded as her eyes grew big. "And he's taking my mommy and me to the movie tonight."

"That's nice," she said as she directed her gaze back to Ben. "I hope you have a good time."

A small smirk pulled at her mouth, and Ben resisted the urge to groan. He knew what she was thinking— the same that everybody else in town who knew them seemed to be thinking—that he and Hannah would be perfect for each other. Maybe so, but he couldn't chance losing her friendship by going there. She'd lost a husband that she loved, and he'd lost a woman who loved him. Neither one of them was ready to move on. He doubted if he ever would be.

Ben smiled. "I'm sure we will," he said as he guided Faith down the hallway to her classroom.

Ten minutes later he was back in his truck and headed home for some much-needed rest after being up all night. The shrill ring of his cell phone startled him, and he saw his office number come up on the dashboard screen. He pushed the button to accept the call.

"Hello."

"Ben, this is Luke."

Ben frowned. "Are you still at the station? You need to go home and get some rest. You were up with me all night."

"I know," Luke said. "I'm getting ready to leave, but I wanted to tell you the latest developments."

"What have you got?"

"The crime scene guys checked for fingerprints on Hannah's car but only found hers."

Ben sighed "I expected as much. Hannah said he had on gloves."

"Yeah," Luke said, "but the good news is that when Hannah was struggling with him for the gun, her fingernails cut through the latex. She had DNA under her fingernails. We've already sent it to the state lab but haven't heard anything yet. You never can tell how long it'll take for them to get results back."

"I know." Ben's stomach roiled, and he rubbed his hand over his eyes at the thought of Hannah struggling to the point that she had been able to scratch through the gloves. "Tell the guys to keep me posted if any results come in, and you get some rest."

"Will do. You do the same."

"I'm on my way home now. I'll check in with you later."

All the way back to his house, Ben couldn't get his mind off what had happened yesterday. When he switched off the engine in his driveway, he gripped the steering wheel with his hands and laid his head down on them. The thoughts of how close Hannah had come to being killed yesterday raced through his mind, and he almost groaned aloud. He couldn't forget how terrified he'd been when his bullet had hit the tire of her car and caused it to drive off the road. As he'd watched it crash into that tree, he'd known he would never forgive himself if he was the cause of Hannah's death. It was bad enough he had to live with the responsibility for what happened to Laura. He couldn't add to the guilt he carried.

After a few minutes he got out of the truck and went inside the house. Suddenly he felt exhausted. He stumbled to his bedroom and collapsed on the bed with a sigh. He'd thought on the way home he was too tired to sleep, but as he closed his eyes and tried to erase the events of yesterday from his mind, he felt himself drifting off.

Sometime later he gasped and sat up straight in his bed. His heart pounded, and a feeling of panic filled him. He rubbed his eyes to rid himself of the dream that had awakened him, but it was impossible to erase the picture in his mind.

In the dream he'd seemed to relive every minute of the chase yesterday. He'd seen his hand gripping the gun and heard himself praying before he fired. Instead of hitting the tire, however, the bullet had shattered the back window of Hannah's vehicle, which had then run off the road. And when he'd run to Hannah, he'd discovered that the bullet he had fired had hit her and killed her instantly. But as he had looked down at her lifeless body, it hadn't been Hannah lying there. It was Laura.

That's when he had awakened.

Now he sat on the edge of his bed, his elbows on his knees and his head buried in his hands. His shoulders shook, and he gasped for breath.

It might have only been a dream, but it felt like the truth. He was the reason Laura was dead. He couldn't let something like that happen again.

If there really was someone who had a vendetta against Hannah, he had to make sure that her assailant wasn't successful the next time. As long as he was alive, Ben vowed he would protect Hannah and Faith. He would do everything in his power to keep them safe, even to the point of laying down his own life if necessary.

FIVE

As Ben pulled to a stop in front of her house that night, Hannah glanced over her shoulder at Faith, who'd fallen asleep in the back seat of his extended cab truck. She smiled and swiveled to face Ben.

"Thank you for taking us to the movie. Even though she's not awake to tell you, I know that Faith had a wonderful time."

Ben switched off the truck and nodded. "I just hope she doesn't have a stomachache tomorrow from all she ate."

Hannah laughed. "That was your fault. You can't seem to tell her no. If all that candy and popcorn makes her sick, I'm calling you to come play nursemaid."

Even in the dim light of the truck Hannah could see his eyes soften. "I'll do anything for her that I can."

Before she could answer, a whimper came from the back seat, and she twisted to see Faith rubbing her eyes. "Mommy, are we home?"

"We are," she answered. "I'll get you out of your seat, and we'll get you inside to bed."

She climbed out of the truck, but before she could

open the back door, Ben was there unbuckling Faith from her car seat and pulling her into his arms. She clasped her fingers at the back of his neck and laid her head on his shoulder.

His dark eyes stared at Hannah over Faith's head. "I'll take her inside. You can get her car seat out."

Hannah grabbed the car seat and followed Ben up the front steps to the house. She unlocked the door, entered and dropped the car seat in the hall. Ben didn't stop, but continued up the stairs toward Faith's bedroom.

It suddenly dawned on Hannah that Ben had carried Faith upstairs on many nights when they'd been to some event and she'd fallen asleep on the way home. She didn't remember Shane ever doing that, or even showing her any attention for that matter. And yet Ben did it as if it gave him great joy.

Hannah followed Ben into the bedroom and watched as he carefully laid Faith on her bed. He stared down at her for a moment before he turned and smiled. "I don't know if you'll be able to get her awake enough to get her pajamas on."

"I've had lots of practice," Hannah responded. "I'll see you out and come back up to get her tucked in."

They didn't speak again as they went back downstairs. When they stopped at the front door, she reached for the doorknob, and Ben turned to face her. "Thank you again for a wonderful night," she said.

His gaze traveled over her face before he replied. "I enjoyed the night, too. Spending time with you and

Faith gives me great pleasure. I hope you know that I would do anything for the two of you."

A lump rose in Hannah's throat, and she stared at him a moment before she spoke. "Ben, why are you so good to us? It seems that as the days go by we take up more and more of your time. I don't want us to cause you to neglect other areas of your life."

He chuckled and shook his head. "Outside of my job, you and Faith are the most important part of my life. I promised Shane I would look after you."

Although she knew his words were spoken with concern and affection for them, she couldn't help but feel a bit disappointed. "You aren't bound to any promise you made to Shane." With so much at stake—hers and Faith's lives on the line—it suddenly felt dishonest to hide from Ben the truth about her relationship with Shane. Finally, she let herself say the words she'd kept inside for so long. "In fact, I don't know why he would even ask such a thing. He never tried to take care of us, so why should he place that responsibility on you?"

Ben's eyes grew round, and he frowned. "What are you talking about? Shane told everybody he knew how much he loved you and Faith. His family meant everything to him."

A bitter laugh rolled from Hannah's throat. "Shane was always focused on making himself look good in other people's eyes. He wanted the reputation of being a devoted husband and father, but nothing could have been further from the truth."

Ben took a step toward her as if he wanted to offer some kind of comfort but then stopped. "You hinted the other night that you had secrets, but I didn't think it was anything like what you're suggesting now."

"I'm not suggesting anything, Ben," she said. "I'm flat-out telling you that Faith and I were never a priority for Shane. I lost count a long time ago of the number of women he was involved with during our marriage. He never fooled around when he was home because he wanted to be the local hero, but you know he wasn't here very much. He was on the road all the time, and he had his pick of groupies."

Ben's Adam's apple bobbed as he swallowed. "If he behaved himself at home, how did you know what he was doing?"

"The first time a woman called here wanting to speak with him, I believed him when he said it was one of the students in the conference class he'd taught. As time went by, the truth got impossible to ignore. Phone calls, notes in his pockets, charges to our credit card. It didn't take long to figure out what was going on. I was reaching the end of my rope when he was killed."

Ben was silent for a moment before he reached out and took her hand in his. "I'm sorry I didn't know, Hannah. I wish I could have helped you."

"Nobody could have help me. I made the choice to marry him even though I knew women threw themselves at him. I just thought he loved me enough to be faithful to me. Unfortunately, all he wanted was the facade of a family and a home."

Ben shook his head, still looking stunned. "I can't believe I didn't see any of this."

"It's not your fault," Hannah assured him. "He

worked hard to keep up appearances, especially with you. Having the local sheriff as a friend only enhanced his reputation."

"This has come as quite a shock to me, Hannah. I don't know what to say."

"You don't have to say anything. I just wanted you to know that I'm not going to hold you to a promise that you made to a man who wasn't honest with you. You need to get on with your own life. I don't want you to feel obligated to us because of a promise you made years ago."

"I'm not obligated," he growled, "and I don't want you thinking that way. We're friends, and friends take care of each other. So don't let me hear you talk like this again."

The sincere expression on his face made her heart prick, and she smiled. "Thank you, Ben. We're fortunate to have a friend like you." Without thinking, she raised on her tiptoes and kissed him on the cheek. She felt his body grow tense when her lips touched his face, and she stepped back from him. "Good night, Ben. I'll talk to you tomorrow." His eyes seemed to bore into hers as he stared down at her before his rough voice answered. "Talk to you then."

He turned and walked out the door and down the steps without looking back. She waited until he had started the truck and pulled away before she closed the door and locked it. Her arms curled around her waist, and she slumped against the door. What had made her do that? She had kissed his cheek without thinking. Had he been offended?

Her cheeks burned, and she knew they must be flushed. How could she face Ben tomorrow or any other day? Through the years he'd told her many times that he didn't plan to ever get serious over a woman. It had something to do with a failed romance when he was in college, but he'd never given her the details. Evidently, it had wounded him badly and made him reluctant to ever have another relationship.

Now he probably thought she had crossed a line. She wouldn't be surprised if his interest in her and Faith lessened and his visits became more infrequent. After a moment she shook her head. She couldn't worry about that. She would explain to him tomorrow that she had simply been conveying her gratitude for all he did for them.

On that thought she walked upstairs and back to Faith's room. She lay just where Ben had placed her, still fast asleep. Hannah propped her hands on her hips and stared down at her daughter for a few moments before she went to the bureau and pulled out a clean pair of pajamas. A bath would have to wait until the morning. For now, she just wanted to get Faith in bed.

Five minutes later, the little girl was tucked in with her arm wrapped around the stuffed bunny she slept with each night. Hannah bent over and placed a kiss on her daughter's forehead before she turned on the night-light beside the bed and walked over to the door. She hesitated before stepping into the hall and glanced back at her daughter before she turned off the overhead light and headed to her own bedroom.

A long, hot soak in the tub would feel good tonight,

but she was so tired. With that thought, she changed into her pajamas and robe, snuggled up in the over-stuffed chair that sat near the window and picked up the devotional book she read from every night before going to sleep.

Fifteen minutes later, she closed the book and bowed her head to pray. At first the words wouldn't come to her because tonight her thoughts seemed to focus on Ben and their friendship. She'd been honest when she told him that she wanted him to live his own life, but she knew she'd miss him if he suddenly found other interests that might take him away from her and Faith.

With a sigh she forced herself to concentrate on the things in her life that she was thankful for. After she'd finished, she turned out the light and climbed into bed.

She had no idea how long she'd slept when the sound of breaking glass roused her. For a moment she thought she must have dreamed it. Then she heard the sound of someone moving about downstairs. Her heart jumped into her throat as she realized that someone was in the house.

Her cell phone lay on the table by the bed, and she grabbed it as she stood. Moving as quietly as she could, she tiptoed from her room into Faith's. Once she was inside, she scooped up her daughter and started toward the door but stopped at the creak on the staircase. Someone was coming up the steps.

Her heart pounded in her chest, and she tightened her arms around Faith as she frantically looked around for an escape route. There was only the one staircase, and she couldn't go there. She doubted if she could hold on to Faith securely enough for them to climb out the window. The closet seemed the best option. She rushed to the closet, stepped inside and closed the door after them.

Faith stirred, opening her eyes. "Mommy," she said, "what's wrong?"

Hannah rubbed her hand over her daughter's hair and hugged her tight. "Nothing to worry about, darling, but I need you to be quiet. Don't talk until I tell you to. I'm going to call Ben, and we're going to hide here until he comes. Can you be quiet?"

Faith nodded. "Are we playing hide-and-seek with Ben?"

"Something like that," Hannah answered as she tucked Faith into the corner. "No matter what happens, don't move. Okay?"

"Okay," Faith whispered.

With trembling fingers Hannah lifted her cell phone and dialed 911. An operator answered immediately.

"Nine-one-one. What is your emergency?"

"This is Hannah Riley. I live at 398 Willow Creek Road. There's someone in my house. I heard glass breaking, and now I can hear him moving around, coming upstairs."

"Where are you now?"

"My daughter and I are hiding in an upstairs closet."

"Help is on the way, ma'am. Stay where you are until they get there and stay on the phone with me."

"Okay."

Hannah pressed her ear against the door in an effort to hear any movement, and her heart leaped when she heard a door open nearby. He was checking out the bedrooms. How long would it take for him to find their hiding place?

"He's close," she whispered into the phone.

"Don't reveal yourself," the operator said. "Officers are about three minutes away from your house."

Three minutes? She and Faith could both be dead before they got here. She needed to find a weapon, but in the dark closet she couldn't see anything. She placed her hand on the floor and began to slide it around in hopes of touching something useful. Her hand brushed against the bat Faith had used when she played T-ball the summer before. It might not be as heavy as a regular baseball bat, but it could still offer some protection, especially if she was able to catch her attacker by surprise.

She tensed as she heard footsteps approach the door to Faith's room and then move inside. She could make out the sound of footsteps on the hardwood floor. Then they stopped.

Hannah held her breath and pulled the phone closer to her mouth. "I can hear him. He's in the bedroom where we're hiding."

"Stay hidden. Officers are one minute away."

Hannah was about to respond when the closet door was suddenly jerked open. In the dark she couldn't make out his features, but as soon as he spoke, she knew it was the same man who had abducted her the day before. He held a gun and pointed it at her.

"Well, well, Mrs. Riley. We meet again. How about you come out and say hello."

The operator's voice called out to her from the phone. "Hannah, what's going on?"

Hannah had no time to answer. She had to protect Faith. "Get away from us!" she hissed.

He tilted his head to one side, glanced down at the phone and laughed. "A lot of good that's going to do you. Now, come out of there before I drag you out."

Before Hannah could answer, Faith stirred in the corner. "Is Ben here, Mommy?"

The man's head jerked around, as he noticed her daughter huddled in the closet. "Well, what do we have here?" He aimed the gun at Faith and then looked back at Hannah. "If you don't want your daughter hurt, you'll come out right now."

A rage filled Hannah. Her mother bear instincts roared to life, and she shouted at the top of her voice. "Get away from my daughter!"

The man took a step back in surprise as Hannah lunged from the closet, the bat raised over her head. With all the strength she could muster, she brought it down on his arm. He bellowed in pain, and the gun dropped to the floor as he took another step backward. But Hannah didn't intend for him to escape. Swinging the bat again, she pushed into the room.

This blow struck the man in the stomach, and he doubled over in pain. The next swing hit him on the shoulder, and he howled in protest. "Get away from me!" she yelled over and over as he stumbled into the hallway with her following.

The sudden sound of sirens split the air, and the man glanced over his shoulder. He grabbed his injured arm and turned back to glare at her. He took a step toward her, but she raised the bat again.

He gritted his teeth and hissed at her. "This isn't the end, Hannah. I'll be back."

With that, he turned and ran from the room. His hurried footsteps clattered on the stairway, and Hannah watched from the upstairs landing as he ran toward the kitchen. The back door slammed shut just as the headlights of a police cruiser turned into the driveway. Only then did she run back to the closet, drop down beside Faith and wrap her arms around her.

As she sat there trembling, she heard the front door crash open and then running footsteps on the stairway. "Mrs. Riley," a masculine voice called out. "We're from the sheriff's department. Where are you?"

She tried to speak, but no words would come out. She cleared her throat and tried again. "In here," she called out.

The next thing she knew, two officers were standing at the doorway. "Where is he?" one of them asked.

"He went out the back door."

"I'm on it!" one of the officers called out as he ran from the room.

The other one knelt and faced her. "Let me help you up."

He reached for Hannah, but she tightened her hold on Faith. He then placed his hand on her arm and helped her to her feet. Her knees threatened to collapse, but he didn't let her go as he led her to Faith's bed and eased her down to sit on it, while asking if either of them was injured and if they needed an ambulance. Hannah confirmed that they were fine, just shaken.

"Everything's all right now, Mrs. Riley," he said. "You and your daughter are safe."

Hannah hugged Faith to her chest and laid her cheek on the top of her daughter's head. They were safe for now, but what about the future? She couldn't get the man's last words to her out of her mind.

"This isn't the end, Hannah. I'll be back."

Ben glanced down at the speedometer and floored the accelerator as he sped through the night with the blue lights on his truck flashing. When dispatch had called, he'd groaned at the thought that he might be called out just when he was getting ready for bed.

His aggravation and fatigue disappeared instantly when he heard that an armed intruder had broken into Hannah's house and that officers were on the way. He'd run from the house and was peeling out of his driveway before the dispatcher had finished giving him the details. He tightened his grip on the steering wheel. If any harm came to Hannah or Faith tonight, he would never forgive himself.

His heart pounded in his chest as Hannah's house came into view. Two squad cars sat in the front yard, their blinking blue lights sending the message that this was a crime scene. He swallowed his fear as he skidded to a stop behind one of the vehicles. He was out of his truck and running toward the house before the engine had completely died.

He leaped up the steps and barreled through the

front door. Two deputies in the entry turned in surprise when he entered. "Where's Hannah?" he demanded.

"In there," one of them responded as he pointed toward the living room.

He turned to enter the room but stopped at the sight of Hannah sitting on the couch with Faith wrapped in her arms. At the sound of his footsteps Faith pulled her head out from where she'd burrowed into her mother, jerked free and ran to him with her arms outstretched.

"Ben!" she cried.

In one swift move he reached down and scooped her up into his arms. She pressed her face into his neck, and he could feel her hot tears on his skin. His arms tightened around her as he walked toward Hannah.

Faith didn't let go of her hold on him as he eased down next to Hannah. He let his gaze travel over her face, and his stomach clenched at how pale she looked. He reached his hand out to her while keeping the other arm wrapped around Faith, and Hannah grabbed hold as if he had become a lifeline.

"Are you all right?" he asked.

She nodded. "I'm fine, just a bit shaken up, but I'll be okay."

Faith pulled away from him enough to stare up at him. "A mean man tried to hurt Mommy and me, but she hit him with my bat and he ran."

Ben's eyes grew wide as he stared at Hannah. "You hit him with a bat?"

She bit down on her lip and ducked her head. "I couldn't let him hurt us. So I did what I had to do."

"Good for you," he said and was rewarded by a

slight smile. Footsteps sounded in the hallway, and he looked toward the door to see Luke standing there. He could tell by the look on his face that he needed to talk to him. "If you're okay, I'm going to talk to the deputies who are searching the scene. I won't be gone long."

Hannah gave a nod, and he kissed Faith on the head before he eased her onto her mother's lap. He rose and walked toward Luke who led him toward the kitchen. The first thing Ben saw upon entering the room was glass lying on the floor in front of the back door where the intruder had broken in.

"He broke the glass, reached in and turned the lock. We've also recovered the gun he used, but we've tried not to touch anything else until the crime scene guys get here to lift prints. I'm sorry to say, we probably won't find any this time, either. Hannah said he wore gloves."

Ben swallowed and tried to concentrate on what Luke was saying, but his heart was still pumping like a drum. "Anything else?"

"He left some footprints outside. We'll take some casts and see if they match the ones found at the site of the wreck yesterday, but I suspect they will. How long do you think it will take for the DNA results to come back?"

Ben shrugged and shook his head. "I don't know. It all depends on how backed up they are. They have to do all the testing before they can search the national database. It could take weeks to hear anything."

"And this guy could do a lot of damage during that time," Luke said.

Ben didn't answer for a moment before he said, "You're right. This guy seems to be serious—and he's not giving up. I know we're short-handed, but I'm going to need a unit outside her house for the rest of the night. Then tomorrow we'll see what needs to be done to keep her safe."

Luke nodded. "I'll take care of it."

"I'm going back to talk to Hannah some more."

Before he could get out the door, he heard Luke on the phone ordering a unit to keep watch outside the house for the rest of the night. That would do for now, but something had to be done to keep Hannah and Faith safe in the future.

When he walked back into the living room, he was surprised to see Hannah alone. "Where's Faith?"

She glanced up at him, a worried expression on her face. "A female deputy arrived while you were gone. I asked her to take Faith up to my room so I could talk to you without upsetting her. I don't want her sleeping in her room alone tonight."

Ben sat down by her and reached for her hand. "I doubt this guy would be stupid enough to come back tonight, but just to make sure I've ordered a unit to stay outside until morning. Then we can decide what we're going to do to keep you and Faith safe."

Tears filled her eyes, and she gripped his hand tighter. "I don't know if I'll feel safe again until this man is caught. I keep hearing what he said about payback. I know he must hate me a lot, but I can't figure out why. There's nothing about him that is familiar. So I doubt that I've met him in the past."

"Maybe it has to do with someone else. Have you had any problems with any of your students?"

Hannah shook her head. "No. Most of them I've known for years. I've recently added some students who are new to this area, but I haven't experienced any problems."

"When are you teaching your next class?"

"Tomorrow. I have a new student coming in the morning to work on target practice and desensitizing his horse. Then I have my regular classes with the younger kids after school tomorrow afternoon."

Ben frowned. "Can you put that off?"

"I'd hate to do that to the kids. They have already paid for the time. I've prided myself on the fact that I follow through on what I promise."

He thought for a moment. "Okay. What time is the first class?"

"It's at ten."

"Then I'll be here, too. In fact, I'll be here earlier because I'm going to have Terry Gray and his crew out here in the morning to put in a security system for you. So, I'll meet them here, then come back and watch you teach your class."

Hannah shook her head. "You don't have to contact Terry. I can do that myself."

Ben scooted closer to her and stared into her eyes. "I know you can, but I'm going to see that he puts in the best system that he's got. We've worked together before, and I know what I want you to have. Do you have anything else to do tomorrow?"

"Valerie is picking Faith up from school at twelve

o'clock, and I was planning to meet them for lunch at the Wagon Wheel. Faith loves their ice cream, and after tonight I think she deserves a treat."

"So you're going to send her to school tomorrow? She's had quite a scare tonight. It might be a good idea to let her stay home tomorrow," Ben said.

Hannah's eyes softened as her gaze traveled over his face. She placed her hand on his cheek. "You're always thinking of us, Ben. I keep telling you that you are too good to us, but I have to confess I'm very thankful for you."

"As I am for you."

Neither of them spoke for a moment, and then he stood and pulled her to her feet. "Why don't you go on to bed? You're safe now, and you can decide whether or not to send Faith to school in the morning. There are two officers outside, and they'll make sure no one bothers you again tonight."

Tears filled her eyes. "But what about tomorrow night and all the nights after that? Last night someone was watching my house, and tonight a man broke in. What am I going to do, Ben?"

A shocked look spread across Ben's face. "You didn't tell me someone was watching your house last night. Where was he?"

"Near the barn. I saw him in the shadows, and then he disappeared."

He inhaled a deep breath and closed his eyes for a moment. Then he placed his hands on her shoulders and stared down into her face. "You should have told me. I would never have left you here alone tonight if I'd known that."

Her lips trembled, and she nodded. "I'm sorry, Ben. I won't do that again."

After a moment he put his arm around her shoulders and led her to the stairs. "I'll tell the officers outside about this, and they'll keep a close watch tonight. Now go on and get in bed. I'll see you in the morning."

She nodded and then climbed the stairs to the second-floor landing. She stopped at the top, looked down at him and smiled before she walked to her bedroom.

Ben watched her go, and her questions rolled around in his head. How was he going to protect her? He'd been a lawman long enough to know that when a criminal was intent on doing harm, there was nothing you could do but wait to see what he would try next.

For now, that was all he could do. Wait to see what else this guy had planned for Hannah and Faith and pray that he would be able to stop him before it was too late.

SIX

Hannah had been running on autopilot ever since she got out of bed this morning. She'd known that Faith would not want to go to school, and she'd given in because of how frightened she had been the night before. Valerie was staying with her so Hannah could teach the student she had coming at ten o'clock.

Right now, though, she couldn't seem to remember what she'd come into the tack room to get. She stood in the middle of the room looking around, hoping something would jog her memory. She heard movement behind her and turned to see her foreman, Dusty, watching her with a wary expression on his face.

"Are you okay, Hannah? I know you had a rough night. I'm sorry Maria and I slept through all the commotion and weren't there to help you, but if you'd like, I can take over your lesson if you need some time for yourself. I'm not the archer you are, but I can help this guy with desensitizing his horse."

Hannah studied the man who'd been her grandfather's employee for as long as she could remember.

When she was a child, she'd followed him around every time she visited the ranch. He was her first idea of what a cowboy should be, and his grizzled appearance only added to that notion as he'd aged.

When her grandfather had died, she'd been afraid Dusty and Maria might leave, but they had let her know right away that they considered this ranch their home, and they would help her keep the ranch running smoothly, and profitably. So they'd stayed on in the small house near the pond on their property. With Dusty's help Hannah had been able to develop a prosperous horse breeding and training program that let her keep an eye on the ranch while focusing most of her time on her real passion—training her students. A few years ago she would never have believed that she would be a much sought after instructor. Her reputation had spread, and that was why she'd been asked to compete in Korea. She owed Dusty a lot for his support.

This morning his gray eyes held concern for her. She smiled and shook her head. "I'm okay, Dusty. Working is the best thing for me right now. It doesn't give me time to think about what happened last night."

Dusty nodded. "That may be best. I'll be in the barn when you need me."

He turned and walked from the room, and Hannah stood there still trying to remember why she'd come in there in the first place. After a moment she shrugged and headed back outside. Just as she emerged from the barn, Ben drove up. She stopped and waited for him to get out of his vehicle. When he did, she smiled. "Good morning."

He studied her face as he walked toward her. "How are you this morning?"

"I'm trying to be better. Haven't made it yet, but I will."

He stopped in front of her and nodded. "I understand. I wanted to tell you I talked with Terry this morning. His crew was planning to spend the day installing a security system in a house that's just been built, but he said your problem was more pressing. He's pulling his crew off that job, and they should be here anytime now to start putting your system in. When they're finished, you're going to have a state-of-the-art system. If anybody tries to get in, it'll light up the whole area around your house, and the signal will come right to our department. You don't have to worry about calling us. Officers will be on their way before you can get to your phone."

"Thanks for taking care of that, Ben. I'll feel a lot safer now."

He let his gaze drift over the barn and the corral before he turned back to Hannah. "Where is Dusty?"

"He's in the barn. We're getting ready for our first client."

A frown pulled at his forehead. "I don't want to alarm you more than you already are, but you need to think before you stand out in the open like this. When I was driving up, I thought you made a good target out here alone."

Her stomach roiled, and she swallowed. "You're right. I'll try to do better, but it's going to be difficult. I do have to teach my classes."

"I know, but…" He didn't finish whatever he was going to say because a truck with a large horse trailer hooked behind pulled into the driveway and drove toward the barn.

"That must be my first student now," Hannah said. She'd spoken with him on the phone, though this was their first meeting in person. All she knew was that he was a recent arrival from Texas who had ridden for several years but wanted to train in mounted archery.

The truck came to a stop a few feet away, and Hannah waited for the driver to get out. When he emerged, her eyes grew large.

He looked like a typical cowboy with his jeans, boots and hat. A braided leather bolo tie hung around his neck, and a silver ornamental clip with a turquoise stone in the center secured it in place. His attire reminded her of other cowboys she'd seen before, but there was something about him that caused the breath to freeze in her chest. His blue eyes sparkled as he walked toward her, and his smile revealed perfect white teeth. She'd never seen a movie star on screen that could rival this man's handsome looks. He held out his hand as he came closer.

"Mrs. Riley? I'm Chuck Murray. I've heard a lot about you, and I'm excited that you decided to take me on as a student. I know I have a lot to learn."

His hand enveloped hers, and she smiled. She felt Ben shift closer to her, and she glanced at him. His eyes had narrowed, and he seemed to be studying the man with a penetrating stare. Turning back to Chuck, she said, "I'm glad to have you at the Smoky Mountain

Mounted Archery Center. As I told you on the phone, we require our clients to have some archery and riding skills before coming. Our techniques will help you merge the two."

He smiled. "And as I told you on the phone, I grew up in Texas, so riding isn't a problem. Archery may be another thing, though. I recently became interested in the sport, so I've been working on target practice a lot. I just hope I can ride a galloping horse without holding the reins and operate a bow at the same time."

Hannah chuckled. "Don't worry about that. You'll probably pick it up in no time."

She felt Ben move closer to her. "What part of Texas did you grow up in?" he asked.

For the first time Chuck seemed to notice Ben. His gaze had been riveted on her ever since he'd climbed from the truck. He glanced at Ben and then to the badge on his chest before he stuck out his hand. "The Panhandle," he said. "I'm sorry I didn't notice you, Sheriff. I guess you heard me tell Mrs. Riley I'm Chuck Murray."

"Ben Whitman," the sheriff said as he shook hands. "What brought you to the Smokies from Texas?"

"I recently sold my start-up business and made quite a bit of money. I visited here once years ago and remembered how beautiful it was, so I thought I'd come back while I decide what I want to do next. I've rented a house with a few acres while I'm here and thought this would be a good time to learn something new. I saw Mrs. Riley's ad in the local paper and thought mounted archery might be something I'd like." He glanced back at Hannah and smiled. "Now that I've met her, I'm glad I contacted her."

Hannah felt her face grow warm, and she glanced at Ben quickly. He didn't appear to find anything amusing about Chuck's statement. If anything, he looked suspicious. Maybe it was his protective nature coming out after what had happened last night.

Ben's eyes narrowed. "I know just about everybody in the county. Whose place did you rent?"

"I don't actually know. I rented it through a vacation rental company—Mountain View Group over at Sevierville."

Ben nodded. "Yeah. I know of them. How long you figuring on staying?"

Chuck shrugged. "I don't know. If I like it here, I may decide to buy something and settle down somewhere around here, but I'd probably want more land than what I have now. I hope to eventually have my own stable, maybe do some training."

"So your family thinks they might like to live here?" Ben asked.

"I don't have a family. I'm single." He flashed a smile at Hannah. "But I'm looking forward to making a lot of new friends while I'm here."

Hannah was beginning to fidget at the way Ben seemed to be interrogating Chuck. She hoped he didn't scare away her new client before she even had a chance to work with him. She cleared her throat.

"We're wasting time standing here talking. Why don't you leave your horse in the trailer for now? Since you're confident in your riding, I'd like to evaluate your archery skills first. After I've done that, I'll get my assistant to help us with your horse."

Chuck tipped his hat. "Sounds good to me. I'll get my bow and arrows."

He turned and walked back toward the trailer. Hannah grabbed Ben's arm. "What's the matter with you?" she hissed. "You sounded like you were interrogating a suspect."

"Hannah, there's a guy out there somewhere who's tried to hurt you twice. Today a man with no ties to this community shows up for a private class with you. I need to make sure that it's safe for you to be around him. I don't want a repeat of what's happened the last two days."

She sighed and rubbed her hands over her eyes. "I don't, either. I'm sorry, Ben. I shouldn't have snapped at you. I just felt very uncomfortable with the way you were questioning him."

"I'm a lawman, Hannah. I question people I'm suspicious of. I'm sorry if it bothers you, but I only have your well-being in mind."

Her chin quivered, and she squeezed his arm. "I know, and I'm sorry. I still haven't recovered from last night."

He nodded. "I understand."

"Are you going to leave then?"

"No, Luke is going to relieve me later, but I'll be here for a while."

With that he turned and walked back toward Chuck Murray, who had stopped outside the barn. If truth be told, she was glad Ben was here. He was right that she knew nothing about Chuck Murray, and it was good to have someone watching out for her.

His statement about Luke coming bothered her, though. She knew Ben's department didn't have the resources to provide around-the-clock protection to all private citizens who were in danger. He'd had two officers stay last night, now he was here and Luke was coming later. She couldn't let him pull his deputies away from their duties to babysit her.

She'd said she wanted to stand on her own two feet and take care of Faith and herself. It looked like that time had come. All she had to do was figure out how she was going to get Ben to let her do that.

Ben leaned against the fender of his squad car and watched as Hannah led Chuck to the practice target. He waited until they were so engrossed in their conversation that he was sure they weren't paying him any mind before he stepped behind Chuck's truck and jotted down the license number. Then he walked back to his car and called dispatch at the office.

Clara, the dispatcher on duty today, answered on the first ring. "Hi, Ben. Where are you?"

Ben grimaced at the sound of her voice. "Clara, I've told you—"

"I know. I know," she interrupted him and then huffed out an exaggerated breath. He could almost imagine how her eyes narrowed as she jerked her glasses off and let them dangle on the chain around her neck. "I'm supposed to say, 'Sheriff's office, what is your emergency.' But that seems ridiculous when I'm perfectly capable of reading caller ID on my phone, and I know how to spell your name. So I assumed that since it was your name and your phone number that it would be you on the line. Now, do you have an emergency?"

A reluctant grin pulled at his mouth, and he shook his head. He should know better than try to tangle with their middle-aged dispatcher, especially on a morning after she'd worked an extra shift last night. He chuckled. "No emergency. I'm sorry, Clara. I wasn't thinking."

"Then, how can I help you?"

He sighed in resignation. "I'm out at Hannah's and—"

Before he could finish, Clara interrupted him again. "How is she this morning? That poor girl has been through enough in the past few days to drive a person crazy. What's wrong now?"

"Nothing is wrong. I just need you to do something for me."

"What?"

"I want you to do a background check on a man named Chuck Murray. I'll text you his license plate number. Then I need one of the deputies to call the Mountain View Group over at Sevierville and find out what they know about him."

"Who is this man?" Clara asked.

"I don't really know," Ben answered. "He's new to the area, and has immediately inserted himself into Hannah's life. Given the timing, I just need to find out something about him. He says he's rented a house and some land from the Mountain View Group. I want to see what they know."

Clara was quiet for a moment before she replied, "We'll get right on it, Ben."

"Thanks, Clara. I'll see you later. I'm going to be at Hannah's place for a while."

"Okay, and tell her I'm thinking about her. I worry about her and that daughter of hers out there all alone on that ranch. And mark my words, it won't be long before she decides that she's safer and happier with a man around the house. And if you're not quick about it, you'll lose your chance for that man to be you. I keep warning you that somebody's going to come along and scoop that girl up right out from under your nose if you're not careful."

Ben sighed and shook his head. "Clara, I don't think this is the time..."

"I'm just saying, Ben Whitman. Don't wait until it's too late."

"Goodbye, Clara. Let me know what you find out about Chuck Murray."

With that, he disconnected the call before she could get the last word in, which was what she was always determined to do. He glanced back at Hannah and Chuck. A slight frown pulled at his brow at how close they were standing to each other. Chuck was bent toward her, his attention directed to the arrow in her hand.

As Ben watched, Hannah glanced up at Chuck then back down as she pointed to the notches at the end of the arrow. Chuck leaned even closer, and Ben felt a momentary pang of resentment. His body stiffened, and he took a step toward them before he realized what he was doing and came to a halt.

There was nothing to be concerned about. Hannah was showing her student the fastest way to nock an arrow, and Chuck had leaned forward to get a better view. That was a skill that Hannah emphasized with beginning horse archers. When competing, there were only fourteen seconds to cover a ninety-meter course. The rider who was the fastest in fitting the string into the grove at the end of an arrow had an advantage.

He walked toward where they were standing and stopped when he could make out what Hannah was saying. "For faster loading of the arrow, I've started using a new method called helicopter nocking."

Chuck appeared engrossed in Hannah's explanation. "What's that?"

She pulled some needle-nose pliers out of her jeans pocket and held the arrow with the notched end up for him to see. "This notch at the end is where the bow's string will fit. I prepare mine like this." As she continued to talk, she demonstrated her actions. "I hold the arrow firmly in my left hand, and with my right hand I place the pliers at a forty-five-degree angle on one side of the notch and bend it backward. Then I do the same on the other side. When the sides are flared out, I press them back together a bit." She then raised the bow and loaded the arrow. "Now when I pull an arrow out of the quiver and line it up, I don't have to position it with my thumb. The arrow rotates, and the string fits down into the notch."

Satisfied that the conversation between Hannah and Chuck was about the lesson, Ben turned and ambled back toward his car. An hour later the two of them walked toward him. As they drew closer, he heard Hannah speak. "I want you to work on nocking the arrow over and over before you come back. I thought we'd have time today to work with your horse, but we'll save that for next time. Your archery skills need a lot of work before you try them from the back of a horse. But even improved skills will do no good if your horse isn't desensitized to the abrupt movement of you pulling an arrow from a quiver and hearing the sound of the arrow hitting a target. You'll be racing around the course, and you won't have hold of the reins, so you have to make sure your horse knows what to do."

They stopped beside Ben, and Chuck shook his head. "When I decided to get involved in this sport, I had no idea there was so much to learn. I don't know if I'll ever learn all of it."

Hannah laughed. "Of course you will. It's not something you learn overnight. It takes a lot of practice and a lot of time."

Chuck looked up at him. "What about you, Sheriff Whitman? Do you participate in mounted archery?"

Ben nodded. "As a hobby. I'm not a professional like Hannah is. We have a small group of people who are interested in the sport, and Hannah serves as our teacher."

"Maybe I can join the group." Chuck stared at him as if challenging him to say no.

Instead Ben shrugged. "That's up to Hannah. She's our leader." His gaze strayed down to the quiver hanging around Chuck's waist, and he tilted his head to one side. "Those are unusual looking markings on your arrows."

Chuck pulled one out and held it up so Ben could get a closer look. "When I decided to get into archery, I heard about this guy in Fort Worth who makes custom arrows. I contacted him, and he makes all mine now. I wanted mine to have a unique marking that would make them easy to distinguish."

Ben nodded. "I know what you mean. When we have a lot of people practicing at one time, it can be tricky to spot ours right away. I just put a splash of yellow color on the shaft of the ones I use, but you have an interesting pattern painted on yours."

"That's because I have Navajo heritage, so I asked him to use a traditional pattern of alternating red and turquoise circles about midway down the shaft."

Ben leaned forward and studied the arrow more closely. "That looks like very good work. I may have to get this guy's name and see about having some made for me."

Chuck grinned. "Just let me know when you're ready, and I'll be glad to oblige. He makes the very best, and when I do anything, I want to have the very best." He turned his attention back to Hannah, and his eyes sparkled. "That's why I came to Hannah. I hear she's a great teacher, and I'm a very willing student."

Ben's skin warmed in aggravation at the veiled flirtatious tone of Chuck's voice, and he glanced at Hannah. A crimson flush covered her face, and his stomach clenched. If Chuck was interested in Hannah, Ben needed to find out about him right away. With all that happened in the past few days, it wasn't wise for strangers to get too close to her right now. Besides, even if she was interested in Chuck, Ben could sense that he wasn't the kind of man she needed.

Hannah smiled and glanced down at her watch. "I'll look for you again the day after tomorrow for another lesson. Until then, if you have any questions, feel free to call me."

"I will," Chuck said. "In fact I may call you even if I don't have any questions."

Hannah's cheeks flushed even brighter, and she cast a quick glance in Ben's direction. "Well, you have a good day."

Ben stepped closer to Hannah as Chuck turned and got into his truck. They stood watching as he drove onto the road and headed back toward town. When the truck was out of sight, Ben turned to Hannah.

"There's something about that guy that troubles me."

Hannah looked up at him, a surprised expression on her face. "What do you mean?"

Ben let out an exasperated breath. "You don't seem to realize the danger you're in. Somebody has attacked you twice. Now a guy you've never seen before shows up, flirts with you, and you seem to enjoy every minute of it."

Her eyes grew wide, and then her expression hardened into an angry mask as she glared at him. "Are you suggesting that I wasn't professional with one of my students?"

Too late he saw how upset she was, but there was no way to take back the angry words he'd spoken. What was the matter with him? Had he begun to feel that his friendship with Hannah gave him the right to judge her actions?

He closed his eyes for a moment and let out a long sigh. "I'm sorry, Hannah. Of course I know you are always professional. Forgive me for what I said. It's just that these attacks on you really have me worried. I guess I'm suspicious of everyone who comes around you."

She didn't say anything for a moment and then nodded. "I don't want us to argue, Ben, so I accept your apology. I promise you that I'll be careful, but Chuck is paying me for lessons. I have to interact with him."

"I know that. I'm only trying to protect you."

"I know," she said, "but I can't put my life on hold. I have students to teach and a ranch to run. I can't stay in my house and hide."

Her voice became louder the longer she talked, and Ben could see that she was getting agitated. He considered asking her to calm down, but he feared it would upset her more. Instead he sighed and nodded. "I understand. Don't worry. We're going to get through this. We'll catch this guy, and then life can go back to normal. Now let's go back to the house and wait for the crew to come with the security system."

"I think that would be a good idea."

She turned and walked back toward the house. After a moment Ben followed. He'd taken only a few steps when his phone rang. He stopped and pulled it from his pocket.

"Hello."

"Ben, this is Luke. I've got the information you requested on Chuck Murray. I called the Mountain View Group over at Sevierville, but they didn't know much about him. He contacted them online about a house they had advertised, and he rented it for four months. They said he told them when he moved in that he was looking for some property in the area to buy. All they know is that he pays his rent on time and they've had no trouble with him."

"I didn't expect them to. How about the background check? Anything on that?"

"Yeah. He's got a record for domestic violence."

Ben tensed and glanced at Hannah who was now entering the house. "What happened?"

"I don't have the case file, just the info from his prison record. He was found guilty of domestic violence four years ago. He served two years in prison and has been out two."

"Do you know who his victim was?"

"Not yet. I'm still working on it."

"You do that. I want to know who his victim was, what he's been doing for the last two years, and where he got his money to move here and rent the property where he's living. He mentioned that he sold a start-up—find out if that's true, and exactly what type of business he was in."

"You got it. I'll let you know as soon as I know anything."

Ben disconnected the call and slipped his phone back in his pocket. Maybe his first impression of Chuck Murray hadn't been too far off base. For now, he didn't want to tell Hannah what he'd found out until he had more information, but he would certainly be watching Hannah's new student.

SEVEN

The next day Hannah was still mulling over her conversation with Ben from the day before. She understood his concern for her, and she was thankful for it. She knew she was in danger. One minute she'd been filling her car with gas, and the next she was speeding down the highway with an armed assailant threatening her. The fact that he'd tracked her to her home and endangered Faith still made her shake every time she thought of it.

Ben was doing all he could to find the man responsible, but so far there were no leads. The investigation could go on for months without determining the identity of her attacker. With her nerves on edge already, she didn't know how she could continue to go about her everyday life as if nothing was the matter. She had to stay strong for Faith, but at the moment her resolve seemed to be hanging by a thread.

She took a deep breath and walked into the barn. All her lessons were finished for the day. Valerie and Faith were inside having a snack that Maria had fixed for them. Dusty had gone into town to get some V-mesh wire for replacing the old fencing in the large pasture behind the barn.

She ambled down the barn's alleyway and stopped at Dixie's stall. This was the horse she'd had since she was a young girl, the one she'd learned to ride on and the one she'd trained and ridden in competitions until Shane ended that part of her career. Dixie was too old now to compete and had been replaced by the younger Blaze, who was her offspring, but Hannah still liked to ride her whenever she had a chance.

Dixie stuck her nose out over the top of the stall's gate and whinnied at her presence. Hannah reached up and rubbed her hand down the mare's face. "I know you wish you were going with me to Korea, old friend, but you've earned your time to rest. Blaze has to take your place, but we'll be thinking of you."

She stood there a moment stroking the horse. The memories of the days when she and Dixie were competing flitted through her mind, and she smiled. Suddenly a thought struck her.

"How would you like to take a practice run on the course?"

As if she understood, Dixie nodded.

Hannah laughed. "Then let's get you saddled."

Twenty minutes later Hannah led Dixie out of the barn. She stopped and adjusted her quiver of arrows around her waist and held her bow as she mounted her horse and turned her toward the practice course at the back of her property.

As she rode toward the course, she had the thought

that she hadn't told Valerie or Maria where she was going. She pulled her cell phone from her pocket and hit speed dial for the house phone. Maria answered right away.

"Hello."

"Maria, this is Hannah. I finished all my lessons today, so I'm taking Dixie for a run on the course. I should be back in an hour or so."

"Do you think that's wise, Hannah? You know Ben told you to stay close to home."

"I know, but I'll just be at the back of the property. Don't worry. It'll be fine."

"Okay, if you're sure."

But Hannah could tell from the tone of Maria's voice that she didn't like it. Before she could voice another objection, Hannah spoke up.

"Tell Faith I'll see her at dinner. Bye." With that she hung up and nudged Dixie into a trot.

They arrived at the course five minutes later, and Hannah pulled the horse to a stop as she gazed at the triple shot Korean course. It stretched in a straight line for ninety meters from one end to the other. The rider had fourteen seconds to complete the run and shoot at three targets spaced along the route.

The first target sat fifteen meters from the starting line and nine meters above the target barriers. The second one sat forty-five meters away and seven meters above the barrier. The third target was seventy-five meters away, and it rose fifteen meters above the barrier.

She studied the three targets and the colorful rings that determined the rider's score. The yellow bull's-eye yielded five points while the circles that radiated outward awarded four for red, three for blue, two for black and one for white. She took a deep breath. Only yellow on all three was good enough to be a contender for the grand prize.

Slowly she pulled an arrow from the quiver and nocked it in preparation for the first target. The others would have to be drawn while the horse was speeding down the course. She checked to make sure the looped strap that connected the reins to the saddle horn was secure before she released the reins and sat tall in the saddle.

Taking a deep breath, she gave the command, and Dixie surged down the course. Hannah shifted her weight to her left leg, and Dixie responded by moving toward the left side of the course. She released the first arrow, grabbed another from her quiver, loaded again and shot at the second. After finishing the third target, she urged Dixie to a stop at the end of the course.

She patted the horse's neck. "Good girl," she murmured as they turned and headed back down the course. At the third target, she dismounted and walked over to retrieve the arrow. With a frown she saw that it had landed in the blue circle. "Three points," she groaned. "That's not good enough. I think I have some practicing to do."

Hannah mounted again and rode to the second target. She'd just pulled the arrow from the bull's-eye when she heard the thunder of hooves nearby. Startled, she looked toward the tree line at the side of the field just as a horse and rider raced from the forest toward her. For a moment she was too stunned to react, and then she saw the figure hunched in the saddle bearing down on her. It could only be the man who had broken into her home.

In a panic, she turned and ran toward Dixie, hoping to ride away before the man could reach her, but she was too far away. The rider reached Dixie first, and she watched in horror as the man lashed out at Dixie with what looked like a leather belt. The sound of the impact of the leather on Dixie's rump crackled in the air, and Dixie cried out in pain before she bolted and raced in the direction of the barn.

Once Dixie was gone, the rider pulled his mount to a stop and turned to face Hannah before he pulled a bow from his back and loaded an arrow.

Hannah's heart pounded so hard she could scarcely breathe. What was he doing? The question had hardly entered her mind before the man spurred his horse forward, his bow aimed in her direction.

For a moment she couldn't move, and then the reality of her situation hit her. She was standing in the middle of an open field, and a man wielding a bow and arrow was bearing down on her.

There was only one thing to do if she wanted to live. Hannah turned and ran toward the tree line at the edge of the field. If she could reach the trees, she might be able to hide. The hiss of an arrow flying past her caused her to stumble, but she wasn't hit. She regained her footing and ran on as the horse and rider bore down on her.

Ben pulled his truck to a stop in front of Hannah's house and sat there for a moment before he turned off the engine. Hannah was going to ask if he had any news on her attacker, and he didn't. She was going to be disappointed, but he couldn't help it. Nothing had checked out. The assailant had left no fingerprints again, and the DNA results still hadn't come back from the state lab. The only thing they did know was that the footprints at both scenes were the same and were from a cowboy boot, but it was impossible to determine the manufacturer.

He did have some more information on Chuck Murray, though. He'd found out that there were several reports of domestic abuse connected to his ex-wife in Texas. The first two times, Murray had managed to convince his wife not to testify against him, which had left the DA without enough evidence to prosecute. After the third accusation, she had filed a restraining order, and that's when he had broken into the house where she was staying and beat her, leaving her badly injured. That's what had prompted the prison sentence.

From what Ben had been able to find out, however, Murray hadn't been in any trouble since he got out of prison. His story about selling a business checked out, and he appeared to be financially viable for the time being. Ben still intended to keep an eye on him, however. It could be a coincidence that a man with a record for assault just happened to move to the Smokies about the time Hannah's attacker surfaced—but years as sheriff had taught Ben just how rare coincidences truly were.

He let out a long breath, got out of the truck and climbed the steps to the front door. Maria opened the door almost as soon as he knocked. She wiped her hands on her apron and smiled when she saw him.

"Good afternoon, Sheriff Whitman. Come in. I have a fresh pot of coffee in the kitchen."

Ben removed his hat and took a step toward her. "I don't have time for coffee. I just came by to check on Hannah. Is she in the kitchen?"

"No. She called a while ago and said she was going to the course to do some practice runs." Maria glanced down at her watch and frowned. "She's been gone long enough that I expected her back before now. Maybe she's at the barn and hasn't come up to the house yet."

Ben nodded. "She probably is. I'll go down and check on her."

He set his hat back on his head and walked around the side of the house toward the barn. There was no one in sight when he reached the corral. He started to go inside the barn, but the sound of a running horse caught his attention.

Suddenly he spotted Dixie galloping across the field from the direction of the practice course. Hannah was not on her. Ben's heart squeezed in his chest, and he ran to stop the horse. He grabbed for the reins as Dixie slowed and came to a stop beside him. His first thought was that Dixie had bolted at some unexpected sound, leaving Hannah to walk home. But a glance in the direction the horse had come revealed only the empty field.

The thought that Hannah might be hurt or in trouble spurred him to vault into the saddle, turn Dixie and set off at a gallop toward the practice course. As they sped along, he scanned the area in hopes of seeing Hannah. His stomach clenched tighter as they charged toward the practice course, but Hannah was nowhere in sight. It was only as they rounded the corner that led to the starting line of the track that he saw her.

His breath froze in his throat at the sight of Hannah running toward the trees at the edge of the field. Behind her a man aimed the bow in his hands toward her as his horse raced after her. Ben's pulse pounded in rhythm with Dixie's hooves as reality hit him. The arrow might hit her or it might not, but regardless, there was no way Hannah could outrun that horse.

Ben pulled his gun from the holster at his waist and fired at the rider. The bullet whizzed over his head, but spooked the horse enough that he had to sling his bow over his shoulder to grab the reins of his horse and stop it from bolting. Ben fired again, and the man looked from him to Hannah. Out of the corner of his eye Ben saw Hannah reach the trees and disappear into the dark forest. Her attacker glanced in her direction once more before he wheeled his horse around and galloped in the opposite direction.

Ben urged Dixie on, and the mare gathered speed as they pursued the rider. But Dixie was no longer young enough to go at high speed for long, and soon the attacker had increased the distance between them. Moments later, he steered his horse toward the tree line and into the forest. Ben contemplated following but then thought differently.

He ran the chance of injuring Dixie if he rode her into the dark forest. His doubted he'd be able to catch

YOUR PARTICIPATION IS REQUESTED!

Dear Reader,

Since you are a lover of our books – we would like to get to know you!

Inside you will find a short Reader's Survey. Sharing your answers with us will help our editorial staff understand who you are and what activities you enjoy.

To thank you for your participation, we would like to send you 2 books and 2 gifts – **ABSOLUTELY FREE!**

Enjoy your gifts with our appreciation,

Pam Powers

**SEE INSIDE
FOR READER'S
SURVEY**

For Your Reading Pleasure...

FREE!

We'll send you 2 books and 2 gifts
ABSOLUTELY FREE
just for completing our Reader's Survey!

YOUR READER'S SURVEY
"THANK YOU" FREE GIFTS INCLUDE:
- ▶ **2 FREE books**
- ▶ **2 lovely surprise gifts**

PLEASE FILL IN THE CIRCLES COMPLETELY TO RESPOND

1) What type of fiction books do you enjoy reading? (Check all that apply)
- ○ Suspense/Thrillers ○ Action/Adventure ○ Modern-day Romances
- ○ Historical Romance ○ Humor ○ Paranormal Romance

2) What attracted you most to the last fiction book you purchased on impulse?
- ○ The Title ○ The Cover ○ The Author ○ The Story

3) What is usually the greatest influencer when you <u>plan</u> to buy a book?
- ○ Advertising ○ Referral ○ Book Review

4) How often do you access the internet?
- ○ Daily ○ Weekly ○ Monthly ○ Rarely or never

5) How many NEW paperback fiction novels have you purchased in the past 3 months?
- ○ 0 - 2 ○ 3 - 6 ○ 7 or more

YES! I have completed the Reader's Survey. Please send me
2 FREE books and 2 FREE gifts (gifts are worth about $10 retail).
I understand that I am under no obligation to purchase any books, as explained on the back of this card.

❑ I prefer the regular-print edition   ❑ I prefer the larger-print edition
153/353 IDL GMRH   107/307 IDL GMRH

FIRST NAME   LAST NAME

ADDRESS

APT.#   CITY

STATE/PROV.   ZIP/POSTAL CODE

SLI-817-SCT17

up with the attacker anyway, since the other man had the faster horse.

With a disgusted shake of his head, he turned Dixie and rode back to where Hannah had entered the woods. She emerged as he approached and ran toward him. He vaulted from the saddle and opened his arms as he hurried to meet her. With a cry she launched herself at him, and he wrapped his arms around her, cradling her head against his chest. He could feel her tears wetting the front of his shirt.

He stroked her hair and crooned to her in an effort to calm her. "It's all right now, Hannah. I'm here, and he's gone. You're safe."

She shuddered and huddled closer to him. "Oh, Ben. I was so scared. I thought he was going to kill me this time."

He rubbed little circles on her back. "But he didn't. You're okay."

They stood that way for a few minutes as she struggled to regain her composure. "Thank you once again for saving me, Ben," she whispered.

He turned his head so that his cheek rested on the top of her head. The floral scent of her shampoo drifted up, and he closed his eyes and inhaled the sweet smell. His heart still pounded as he thought that he could have lost her today. If he had, he knew his life would never have been the same again. She had become too important to him.

After a moment he pulled away from her, and she looked up at him. He smiled and caressed her cheek. "Are you ready to go home now?"

She nodded. "Yes."

He led her to where Dixie stood waiting patiently. He climbed into the saddle, reached down and pulled Hannah up behind him. She scooted close to the back of the saddle and wrapped her arms around his waist. His heart raced as he reached down and squeezed her hands.

"Are you comfortable?"

He could feel her nod as she laid her head against his back. "Yes, I'll be fine."

But would she? It was clear that this man wasn't going to stop until either he was arrested or Hannah was dead. If Ben wasn't able to track him down, then the next attack could succeed.

EIGHT

Pressed against the comforting bulk of Ben's strong back, Hannah could feel the way his tense body relaxed as they came to a stop outside the barn. Even if her attacker decided to come back for another try at firing arrows at her, they'd be able to reach the safety of the barn before he could strike.

Ben climbed off Dixie first and reached for Hannah to help her down. Still shaking slightly from the aftermath of her fear, she fell into his arms, and he lowered her to the ground. Seeming to sense her need for comfort, he kept his hold on her and they stood there for a moment locked in each other's arms.

Hannah was the first to pull away. She stepped back and stared up at Ben. "Thank you again, Ben. I really don't know what I would have done if you hadn't been there."

He didn't say anything for a moment, just let his gaze travel over her face. It drifted to her lips, and he stilled as if he was hypnotized. He made a small movement toward her, and she knew from the look in his eyes he was going to kiss her. And even though it was something she had never expected, she didn't hesitate before she tilted her head back to give him better access to her lips. But then a soft groan came from his throat. He straightened, took a deep breath and released the hold he still had on her.

"I'm glad I was there," he answered in a flat tone.

Hannah's heart plummeted to her stomach, and her knees wobbled. Had she misread his intentions? And did she want him to kiss her?

Her cheeks burned at the unanswered questions flying through her brain. After a moment she reached for Dixie's reins. "I need to take care of my horse. She's had quite a workout this afternoon."

He only nodded as she turned and walked away. Dusty walked from the barn at that moment and called out to her. "Hannah, where have you been? I saw that Dixie was gone from her stall, and I was worried about you."

She was still too upset to talk about what had happened, so she only smiled. "I'm okay, Dusty, but Dixie has had a rough afternoon, and she's got a cut on her flank that needs attention."

He reached for the reins. "Let me take care of her, and you go on up to the house. You look like you could use a break."

"Thank you, Dusty," she said as she handed him the reins. "I think you're right. I need a good meal, a bath and a good night's sleep."

"Then I'll see you in the morning," he answered as he turned and led Dixie toward her stall.

She waited a moment and took several deep breaths before she turned back to Ben. Finally, she pasted a smile on her face and walked back toward him. "Do you want to come to the house with me?"

"I'll walk back up there and get my truck. Then I'm going to drive over to the practice course. I need to retrieve those arrows."

"Okay. Afterward, do you want to stay for supper?"

He glanced at his watch. "I guess I can stay for a bit. I'd like to see Faith and hear how school went today."

A frown pulled at Hannah's brow as they walked toward the house. "Since I don't have a car yet, I drove her this morning in the ranch truck, and then I walked her to her classroom. I talked with her teacher and told her that we were having some problems, and I'd like for her to keep a close watch on Faith until everything is resolved. She said she would."

Ben nodded. "I think that was wise. What about your car? Can it be repaired?"

She shook her head. "No, it's a total loss. I talked to the salesman at the local dealership. They didn't have a replacement that I wanted, but they've checked around for me. I'm expecting it to be delivered to me tomorrow."

"Good. But after what happened today, I don't think you need to drive anywhere. I can take Faith to school for you."

She was silent for a moment as she recalled the attack that had taken place just a short while ago. "Thanks, Ben, but after today, I may never want to

send her back to school. I don't think I can stand to
have her out of my sight."

Ben stopped and took her hand in his. "You've been
through enough to make you understandably scared. I
wish I could take that away from you, but I can't. All I
can do is promise you that I'm not giving up on finding
this guy. Now that you've got the security system and
I have deputies posted here every night, I feel better
about your security." He grinned and tilted his head
to the side. "That is I *will* feel better if you promise
you won't go off on your own again like you did this
afternoon."

She laughed and nodded. "Don't worry. I've learned
my lesson." The thought of the upcoming competition,
however, caused her to sober instantly. "But I need to
practice if I'm going to make a good showing in Korea.
Winning an event there could go a long way to furthering
my professional standing here in the States. I can't win
if I don't practice, and I can hardly squeeze the practice
course inside the house."

Ben pursed his lips and gave a short nod. "I understand. Just wait until I'm off duty, and I'll go to the
practice course with you."

"That's so sweet of you, Ben. I feel bad about taking you up on your offer, but I need the time on the
course. So I'll agree. But there's one thing that we
need to address."

"What's that?"

"You can't go on having your deputies park outside
my house all night. I know you're short staffed, and

you don't need to tie them up here. Since I have the alarm system, I feel you need to rethink that decision."

Ben shook his head. "It's all right." She arched her eyebrows in a skeptical look, and he frowned. "It's the truth. We've been able to cover everything. Don't worry about it."

"But I do worry," she answered. "I don't want the people of the county thinking you give special treatment to your friends. I want you to relieve your deputies of babysitting duty for me."

He looked at her for a moment before he finally nodded. "I do feel better with the alarm system installed. Maybe I can just have them do some drive-bys during the night."

"That would make me feel better. I don't want anyone to have reason to criticize you because of your concern for us."

He bit down on his lip, and they walked the rest of the way in silence. When they got to the house, she stepped up on the back porch and waited until his truck came around the corner of the house, headed toward the practice course. Then she stepped through the back door and smiled when she spied Valerie and Faith sitting at the kitchen table, their heads together as Valerie read aloud from a book. Maria stood at the stove stirring a pot of stew.

She stood there several minutes surveying the scene before her and saying a prayer of thanks that she had survived the attack earlier. Then Faith looked up, smiled and squealed as she jumped up and ran toward her. "Mommy!" she cried. "Where have you been?"

"Riding," she answered as she scooped Faith up in her arms and hugged her tightly against her body. She looked down at the book on the table. "What are you doing?"

"Valerie is reading me a story."

Before Hannah could respond, Ben walked in the back door. Her gaze drifted over her daughter's head and to Ben's dark eyes. The troubled look told her he was thinking the same thing she was. If he hadn't arrived at the practice course when he did, she wouldn't be with her daughter right now. She would be dead.

Hannah kissed Faith on the cheek and forced herself to release her daughter. "Say hello to Ben. He wanted to find out how your day at school went."

Faith grinned as she launched herself at Ben. She giggled and wrapped her arms around his neck as he caught her up in his arms and lifted her high. When he lowered her, Hannah saw the fierce, protective expression that covered his face, and he frowned as he closed his eyes and swallowed.

After a moment he smiled and released her. "Did you have a good day at school?"

Faith nodded. "I did. Janie Culver likes me again. We played together at recess today."

Ben smiled. "Good. Just remember, always be nice to everyone even when they're being unkind to you. Show that you can be a friend no matter what."

"I will," Faith answered. "Are you staying for dinner?"

"Your mother invited me. I'll stay if you want me to."

She laughed and hugged him again. "I want you

to stay. Better yet, I'd like you to stay with us always here at our house."

A small startled groan escaped Hannah's mouth. "Ben has a house of his own, darling. Now why don't you go with Valerie and get washed up for dinner?"

Valerie rose from where she still sat at the table and held out her hand to Faith. "That's a good idea. Come on with me. We'll go use some of the sweet-smelling soap your mother has in her bathroom."

Faith laughed, grabbed Valerie's hand, and the two hurried from the kitchen. Maria turned from stirring the pot on the stove and stared at Hannah. "I didn't want to ask in front of Faith, but did something happen today? You're getting back later than I thought you would be."

"There was a problem over at the practice course, but Ben took care of it."

Maria opened her mouth to speak but glanced from Ben to her and then sighed. "I need to check on something in the living room before we eat," she said as she reached over and turned off the stove. "I'll be back in a few minutes."

Hannah watched Maria exit before she turned back to Ben. "I think she wanted to give us some time alone. Did you get the arrows?"

"I did."

She waited for him to say more. When he didn't, she prompted him. "And?"

"They had the same markings as the ones Chuck Murray showed me when he was here for his lesson."

Hannah's mouth gaped open. "Do you think Chuck is the man who's attacked me?"

He rubbed the back of his neck. "I don't know. If it was Chuck, it seems strange that he would use arrows with markings like the ones he showed me. I'm going to take the arrows to our crime scene guys and see if they can lift any fingerprints, but I'm leaning toward that conclusion."

"But why? I'd never seen him until he came for his lesson."

"I don't know," Ben said as he took a step toward her, "but what happened this afternoon has me upset."

"Me, too."

"This guy has tried three times to kill you. And today… Who would have thought he'd use a bow and arrow? The way he rode and shot tells me he knows a lot about mounted archery. Chuck said he was a beginner in the sport. So he either lied or it wasn't him. But it must be someone connected to him in some way to have gotten his arrows. He said they were custom made for him, right? So it's doubtful that somebody else marked their arrows just like his. At this point I don't understand what reason Chuck would have to target you. Are you sure you can't think of anyone in the sport who would like to see you hurt?"

She shook her head. "There's no one. I've never had a cross word with anyone that I can remember."

"What about Shane? Did he ever mention any problems with anyone?"

She shook her head. "He never talked about the people he met when he was conducting training sessions or competing. He didn't want to talk about them when he got home."

Ben rubbed the back of his neck and frowned. "This is driving me crazy. I feel like I'm fighting some kind of phantom. He appears, attacks you and then disappears into the shadows. I'm failing you by not finding out who this guy is."

She stepped closer and placed her hand on his arm. "You're not failing me at all. He can't hide forever. You'll get him."

Just as she finished speaking, her cell phone chimed that a text message had just arrived. Then it chimed a second time and then a third. She pulled the phone from her pocket and frowned. "Who could be so insistent to send three texts to me?"

She opened the first one and gasped at a picture of her holding the school door open for Faith to walk inside. It had been taken that morning—she recognized the clothes they were wearing. Underneath there was a message. You can't get away from me. I'm watching all the time.

She gasped, and Ben stepped closer. "What is it?" he asked.

She didn't answer as she opened the second text. This one was a picture of Faith on the playground at recess. She and Janie Culver appeared to be bouncing a ball back and forth between the two of them. The third picture was of Valerie holding the door of her car open for Faith to climb inside. It also had a message underneath. You'd better watch your daughter. It would be so easy to take her.

At that message she gasped, and the phone slipped from her fingers. It thudded to the floor as she covered her face with her hands. Beside her, Ben bent and picked up the phone. There was silence as he straightened. She removed her hands and looked at him.

She could tell he'd looked at the texts. The steely look in his eyes sent fear coursing through her. She'd seen him upset before, but never like this. He speared her with his gaze, and in his determined look she saw the raw truth. She and Faith weren't just some citizens who needed the protection of the sheriff's office. His fierce possessiveness told her that she and Faith were more than just friends to him. They were *his*, and they always would be. And he would do whatever it took to keep what was his safe.

Her eyes grew wide, and her mouth gaped open. The look shocked her not just because it changed the way she viewed Ben, but because it changed the way she viewed *herself.* She'd thought she was through with feelings deeper than friendship for any man in her life, and yet now she knew that had changed. Had it taken threats on her life and that of her daughter for her to fall in love again?

She didn't have all the answers yet, but they would have to wait. First, they had to stop a man who intended to murder her. After he was caught, there would be time to think about her feelings and what the future might hold.

Ben didn't think he'd ever been as angry and frightened as he was when he saw the pictures of Faith on

Hannah's phone. The picture of that sweet child who'd owned his heart since the day she was born had brought out the feeling that he thought a father must experience when trying to protect his child. It was troubling enough to have Hannah in the sights of a killer, but to target a child was the most reprehensible act he could imagine.

He pulled his truck to a stop in front of his office and sat there a minute clutching the steering wheel. He hardly remembered what he'd said to Hannah after he'd seen those pictures. He remembered telling her to send Valerie home and set the alarms. Then he'd made his excuses about having some work to do at the office and had rushed out of there.

Truthfully, he *did* have work to do at the office, but the real reason for leaving was that he wanted to get the arrows to their lab. He needed to find Hannah's attacker, and so far every way he had turned had been a dead end. There were no fingerprints, the DNA results hadn't come back and the other scraps of evidence— shoe prints, clothes, minimal physical descriptions— were too broad to be helpful. But now, he'd found out that Chuck Murray had been in prison and that the arrows used today were similar to the ones he'd seen in the man's quiver. Could that be enough to finally break the case? He climbed from his truck and walked into the station.

Tammy Cross, the nighttime dispatcher, looked up and smiled when he walked in. "Good evening, Sheriff. We didn't expect you back tonight. Is there anything I can do for you?"

"I'm taking some arrows back to the lab. I want them checked for fingerprints."

"Yes, sir. Our techs are at the scene of a robbery right now, but I'll contact them to get on it as soon as they check back in."

"Thanks, Tammy. Is Luke still here?"

She frowned. "I'm not sure. He clocked out about thirty minutes ago, but I haven't seen him leave. He may be around somewhere. Do you want me to see if I can find him?"

"Thanks, Tammy. If you find him, I'll be in my office," he said, as he turned toward his office.

Once inside with the door closed, Ben sank into the chair behind his desk and sighed. He propped his elbows on his desk and covered his face with his hands. He sat that way for a few minutes and thought about everything that had happened today. He'd almost been too late to save Hannah, and the unknown assailant had gotten close enough to Faith to take pictures of her. The fact that he was at her school disturbed him the most. What if he had lured her over and kidnapped her? The thought made him sick to his stomach, and he groaned.

A soft knock at the door brought him up straight in his chair, and he cleared his throat. "Come in."

The door eased open, and Luke stuck his head around the side. "I was just about to leave a note on your desk, but Tammy told me you were back. Do you have a minute to talk?"

Ben stood and motioned for Luke to enter. "Of course. What's on your mind?"

Luke walked in and sat in the chair in front of Ben's

desk. He pulled a notepad from his pocket and flipped the pages as Ben settled back in his chair. After a moment Luke found what he was looking for and glanced up.

"I got to thinking about this Chuck Murray having a record, and I did a bit more investigating today. I talked to the detective in Texas who investigated the domestic violence case. He said he'd seen a lot of victims, but this guy's wife had been beaten within an inch of her life. In fact, it was shocking that she didn't die. He thought the sentence should have been longer, but the judge was the one to decide. Then he said Murray had the warden and all the guards convinced he was a changed man while he was in prison. They all went to bat for him when his parole hearing came up. The detective thought he should still be in jail for what he did, but it didn't work out that way."

Ben exhaled a long breath. "Yeah. Sometimes the justice system doesn't work the way we want it to."

"Anyway," Luke continued, "I asked if Murray's wife still lived in the area. The detective said she moved to Colorado after the trial, but he still keeps in touch with her from time to time. She's remarried now and has a child. He said he was glad she was able to move on because she deserved to be happy."

"That's good for her. What else did he say?"

"He gave me her name and address in case you wanted to talk with her about her ex-husband."

Luke tore a page from his notepad, then reached across and handed it to Ben. "Her name is Leslie Dillard. Her phone number is written below her name."

Ben looked down at the name and nodded. "Thanks, Luke. Good work. I think I'll give her a call." He glanced at his watch. "Colorado is an hour earlier than we are, so it shouldn't be too late to call."

Luke pushed to his feet. "Well, I'll leave you to it. I promised my wife I'd be home for dinner tonight, and I'd like to be on my way."

Ben waved his hand in dismissal. "Go on home. Don't keep that pretty wife waiting."

Luke grinned and pushed up from the chair. He walked to the door but stopped and turned before he opened it. "Have I ever told you how great it feels to know that somebody who loves you is waiting to welcome you home every night?"

"Not in so many words," Ben drawled, "but I get the idea."

"Just saying." Luke swallowed before he continued, "In this job we see a lot of bad things, but having a good woman in your life makes up for all that."

"I'm sure it does," Ben said through tight lips.

Luke reached out and opened the door. "It's something to consider, Ben. You might find you really like it."

Ben didn't say anything as Luke walked out the door. He sat there for a few minutes and thought about what Luke had said. He remembered how scared he'd been when he'd seen that guy chasing Hannah with an arrow aimed at her back. Then later, once he knew they were safe, he'd almost given in to his desire to kiss her.

He couldn't hide the truth from himself any longer. He'd loved her since the day he first saw her when she came to live with her grandfather. Just out of college, she was so young and beautiful, and she'd captured his heart. But then Shane had entered the picture, and he'd had to put his feelings aside and focus on being happy for her. After Shane's death, he'd thought she was grieving too much to ever want to fall in love again, but according to what she'd told him a few days ago, her marriage hadn't been as happy as he'd thought.

It seemed that at the moment there was nothing keeping them apart except the fact that he had no idea whether he could ever commit again. Every time he thought about it, he remembered Laura and the night she'd died because of him. He didn't know if he would ever get past the guilt he felt over her death.

In an effort to shake those thoughts from his head, he glanced down at the phone number for Leslie Dillard. He picked up the phone and punched in the number on the paper. After a few rings, a woman answered.

"Hello."

"Mrs. Dillard?"

"Yes. Who's calling?"

"My name is Ben Whitman. I'm the sheriff in Sevier County, Tennessee, and I'd like to ask you some questions about your ex-husband if you have time."

There was silence for a moment before she replied. "You want to ask me some questions about Chuck? May I ask what he's done now?"

"Nothing that I can prove. His name has come up in an investigation, and I know he spent some time in prison for attacking you."

"Yes," she said, "but not enough time as far as I'm concerned."

"Mrs. Dillard, I don't want to bring up bad memories, but I'd appreciate any information you can give me about him. He's moved to our community, and he's linked to an investigation into the attempted murder of a woman."

A weary sigh rippled over the phone. "It wouldn't surprise me if he's guilty. He's a con man, Sheriff. He can charm you into believing anything he wants you to, but down deep he's as sadistic as they come. I didn't find out what he was really like until after I married him. Then I discovered that all he wanted was the money I'd inherited from my family. He was good to me as long as the money lasted, but when it was all spent, he began to show his true nature. I barely got away from him alive. The last beating he gave me almost killed me."

"That's what I heard, and I'm sorry you had to endure that. I understand you're happy now, though."

"Yes, I'm married to a wonderful man, and we have a beautiful daughter. We enjoy the same things. We are active in our church, and we belong to a mounted archery group that—"

"Mounted archery?" Ben sat up straight in his chair and interrupted her.

"Yes…" she said hesitantly. "We met at a competition. We'd both enjoyed the sport for years, but our paths never crossed."

"Mrs. Dillard, what about Chuck? Did he participate in mounted archery?"

"As a matter of fact, he's the one who introduced me to it. He'd been competing for years when we met. He used to go to workshops and training sessions all the time."

Ben's heart began to race. He licked his lips, almost afraid to ask the next question. "Were you familiar at any time with a man named Shane Riley?"

She gave a little laugh. "Shane? Of course I knew him. He was our instructor several times and even visited our home. He and Chuck were good friends. I don't like to speak ill of the dead, but I never did like that man."

"Why not?"

"Because every time Chuck spent time with him, he'd come home and tell me how Shane had married a woman who had money and a profitable ranch. He'd throw it in my face that Shane's wife gave him all the money he needed, not like me who he claimed kept too tight a hold on the purse strings. He'd say he wished he had a wife like Shane's, not a miser like me. He'd start to drink, and he'd get so angry that no matter what I did, I would end up black and blue before the next morning."

"I'm so sorry, Mrs. Dillard."

She sighed. "When the money ran out and he left, I thought it was over, but it wasn't. He found me again, and that time it was worse than ever. That's when I pressed charges, and he went to jail." She paused for a moment. "You said you're a sheriff in Tennessee. Is Chuck living there now?"

"Yes, he is, and he's passed himself off as being a beginner in horseback archery."

She laughed. "Well, nothing could be further from the truth. If he's saying that, he's running a con game on somebody. Is it a woman?"

Ben closed his eyes and bit down on his lip. "Yes, it's a woman, an instructor."

"Does she have money?"

"She's not wealthy, but she has some money she inherited from her grandfather, and a ranch that's doing well."

"Then he's set his sights on her. Warn her before it's too late. I don't want him to hurt anyone else like he did me."

Ben cleared his throat. "Thank you for talking with me, Mrs. Dillard. You've been a great help."

"I hope I have helped you, Sheriff. Feel free to call me again if you need to. I will do whatever I can to see that Chuck Murray doesn't take advantage of anyone else. Goodbye."

Ben disconnected the call and sat at his desk pondering what he'd just learned. Chuck Murray had just cemented his place at the top of Ben's suspect list. But why would he want to hurt Hannah at this point? They'd just met. If he was running a con game on her, he would have to worm his way into her life before he could get any money. Why would he try to kill her? Could this be some elaborately staged con to make her think she's in danger so that he could then come across as some knight in shining armor riding to her rescue? But how would he do that?

The file with the background check Luke had done on Chuck Murray still lay on the side of his desk. He opened the file and glanced down the page until he found Chuck's telephone number. Ben punched in the number and waited for him to answer.

"Hello."

"Mr. Murray, this is Sheriff Whitman. I met you at Hannah Riley's place when you came for a lesson."

"Yes, Sheriff. I remember. What can I do for you?"

"I wondered if you could come into my office in the morning. I have some questions I'd like to ask you."

There was silence on the other end of the line. Finally, he spoke. "What's this about, Sheriff."

"It's about a case I'm investigating. I thought you might be able to shed some light on a few things."

"Look, Sheriff Whitman, if this is about my record, you can give it a rest. I served my time, and I haven't done anything since I've been here to cause any trouble."

"Did I say anything about you being in trouble?" Ben tried to sound surprised. "I just want to ask you some questions. Say about ten o'clock?"

Chuck didn't answer for a moment. Then he sighed. "All right. I'll come in, but I'm coming under protest. I don't want to get involved in anything that's going on in the area."

"Thank you," Ben said. "I'll see you then."

Before Chuck could respond, Ben hung up the phone. He sat there for a few minutes, thinking about how he would question him tomorrow. After a moment he exhaled and pushed to his feet. This was going to take some thought.

He had no idea what kind of game Murray was playing, but one thing was certain. "I'll be watching," Ben muttered, "and if you think you're going to take advantage of Hannah, you have another think coming."

NINE

Hannah was sitting at the kitchen table having a cup of coffee the next morning when Ben walked in. She looked up and gave a slight frown when she saw him. Even though his handsome features always exuded a professional manner, this morning he looked tired.

"Ben," she said. "I didn't hear you come in."

"Maria let me in. I just wanted to see how you and Faith were doing this morning."

Hannah rose, walked over to the cupboard and pulled out a cup. "Sit down and have a cup of coffee with me. You look like you could use it."

He didn't respond but dropped into the chair and rubbed his hands over his eyes. "I didn't sleep well last night. I kept seeing those pictures of Faith."

She set the coffee in front of him, sat down and picked up her cup. She knew what he meant. Every time she'd tried to shut her eyes last night it seemed that she saw either an arrow aimed at her back or Faith bouncing a ball on the playground. "I know." She wondered if he could hear the fear in her voice.

He looked up from stirring his coffee and stared into her eyes. She'd often thought that Ben had the most beautiful dark eyes she'd ever seen, but this morning there was something else there. He couldn't hide his fear.

She swallowed and let her gaze drift over his face. The lines of worry around his eyes caused her heart to prick. What was going through his mind?

"Ben, what is it?" she asked. "What's wrong?"

He opened his mouth as if to speak but instead pushed his chair back and jumped to his feet. He strode to the window where he stopped and stared outside. His hand raked through his hair. "Yesterday was almost too much for me, Hannah. When I saw that guy aiming an arrow at your back, I thought I was going to be too late to help you. But then, the pictures of Faith…" He stopped, and a choking sound rumbled in his throat. He took a deep breath. "They knocked me for a loop. I can't believe anybody could be low enough to threaten a child. If anything happened to you or Faith, I don't know what I'd do. You're the two most important people in my life."

She hesitated for a moment before she walked over to him and laid her hand on his arm. He flinched at her touch, and she tightened her hold on him. "Ben, look at me." When he didn't turn to face her, she squeezed harder. "Ben, I said look at me."

Slowly he turned. "Hannah…"

She put a finger to his lips to quiet him before she spoke again. "I have to admit that the things that have happened the last few days have scared me. I don't want to be hurt, but I would give up my life to keep Faith from being harmed. I'm so glad you've been here with me. You've protected us and you've encouraged me when I was afraid. You've been my rock when I needed someone to lean on. I thank you for that."

"I haven't done anything—"

Again she interrupted. "But being thankful to you is only a small part of what I feel. We've been friends for a long time, but I feel like the danger that we've shared the last few days has brought us closer together. I feel like there's something changing in our relationship, but I don't know if either one of us is brave enough to admit it and deal with it."

He stared into her eyes for a moment and then raised his thumb and raked it across her bottom lip. "I'll never forget how you looked that day you arrived here from college. I had stopped by and was standing outside the barn with your grandfather when you drove up. When you stepped out of the car, I thought I'd never seen a more beautiful woman. I still think that. When you married Shane, I tried to resign myself to being nothing more than your friend."

She took a deep breath. "And you've been a great friend, but the way you look at me when you think I'm not noticing makes me wonder if what you feel is more than friendship."

"It is more, but I tell myself I'm not the man for you. There are things in my past…"

"I don't care about your past. I care about now. You, me and Faith."

His hands came up, and he gripped her arms. "That's

what matters to me, too, but before I can think about our future, I have to find out who's trying to hurt you."

She nodded. "I understand." She waited a moment and when he didn't say anything, she spoke again. "So where do we go from here?"

He released her arms. "Nowhere for now. Not until you and Faith are safe."

"Okay. But when this is all over, I don't think we'll be able to go back to the way things used to be. I'm through living in the past, and I'm going to make a future for Faith and me either with you or without you. Do you understand?"

"I understand, but until I find the answers we need, I want you to do several things."

"What?"

"First of all, we need to make sure Faith is safe. What are we going to do about school? I don't feel good about sending her for the time being."

"That's already taken care of. I've notified the school of the situation and withdrawn her for the time being. Since Faith will be home all day, I've asked Valerie to move into our guest room. I've warned her that this might put her in danger, too, but she insists she wants to help any way she can, and she's agreed to stay here for a while until this is all over. They're in the den right now."

"That's good. There's one other thing I'd like for you to do." He pulled a piece of paper from his pocket. "This is the website of a company that makes children's clothes with hidden GPS trackers in them. The clothes look like any regular ones that a child would wear. I think it would be a good idea to buy some for her."

Hannah nodded. "I'll do that this morning."

"And I don't think anyone else should know about this. Not Maria, or Dusty, or Valerie. Just the two of us. It's not that the others aren't reliable, but you never can tell what a person will let slip when they're involved in a conversation. One word that reaches the ears of the wrong person can be a disaster."

Her heart pricked as if it had just been pierced by a cold shard of ice. "I won't tell anyone."

His forehead wrinkled, and he frowned. "And there's one more thing. About your lessons."

"What about them?"

"I know you don't want to call them off, but I think you should for now."

"Ben, I've told you…"

He held up a hand to stop her. "I know, but I have some information that changes things."

"What information?"

He took a deep breath. "Chuck Murray hasn't been honest with you. He has spent time in prison for domestic violence. I talked to his ex-wife last night, and she told me that she and Chuck used to compete in mounted archery. So he's not a beginner like he pretended to be."

Hannah's mouth dropped open. "Why would he lie about that?"

"Because Chuck was friends with Shane, who told him all about his wife who had inherited some money and who was running a successful ranch. His ex-wife said Chuck spent all her inheritance, and when the money was gone, he nearly killed her. She described him as a sadistic con man."

"B-B-But I don't understand."

Ben stepped closer. "Don't you see? He'd heard Shane talk about you and your wealth, and he knew Shane was dead. He's on the hunt for money, and he decided to target you."

Hannah placed her palms on her cheeks and stared at him. "I'm so sorry. You were right all along, and I got upset with you."

"It doesn't matter now." He glanced at his watch. "I have a meeting with Murray at ten o'clock, and I intend to get some answers from him. I'll let you know what he says."

"Okay, I can postpone my classes until I get back from Korea. I'll tell my students I need time to prepare for the international competition that's coming up in a few weeks."

His eyes grew wide, and he looked at her as if he couldn't believe what he'd heard. "You're still planning to go to Korea after everything that's happened?"

She nodded. "Yes. I need to do this, Ben. Please understand."

His lips pulled into a grim line, and he finally nodded. "Okay, but I'm going with you. I already have a passport. Do I need to take care of anything else? Immunizations? Visa?"

She shook her head. "A passport is all that's needed. Although there aren't any immunizations required, I want to make sure all of Faith's shots are up to date."

He nodded. "Good idea. I'll start making my plans, because I'm not letting you and Faith get that far away from me again."

She smiled. "I'm glad. I've asked Valerie to go, too. Maybe we can get away to do some sightseeing while she watches Faith."

He reached up and cupped her face with his hand as his gaze drifted over her face. "I'd like that very much."

The sound of footsteps at the door caught their attention, and they looked up to see Valerie standing there. Her face flushed when she saw them standing so close. "Excuse me," she muttered. "I didn't mean to disturb anything."

Ben stepped back from Hannah, and she smiled at Valerie. "You're not. Do you need something?"

"I was wondering if it would be all right to take Faith outside. It's a beautiful day, and she needs some exercise. I'd keep her right at the swing set and wouldn't let her out of my sight."

"That's fine, Valerie. We have to try to make life as normal as possible for her."

Valerie nodded and turned back to the den. When she was no longer in sight, Ben cleared his throat. "I have to go. Chuck Murray will be waiting."

She nodded. "Okay."

He started to turn away, but then he stopped. He stared down into her eyes, then leaned forward and kissed her cheek. "I'll see you later," he whispered.

Hannah could only nod as he walked away. After a moment she sank into her chair at the table. She folded her arms on the table and laid her head on them. What was she thinking? She had as much as given Ben an ultimatum to decide if he wanted to either share a life with her and Faith or get out completely.

After a moment she raised her head and smiled. He hadn't rejected the idea. Instead he'd insisted he was going with them to Korea. That made her think he might be ready to explore the next phase of their long friendship. She hoped so because she knew she was.

Ben tried to be patient as he waited for Chuck Murray's appointment, but he couldn't help feeling a bit anxious. The things he'd learned about the man last night concerned him, especially since he suspected Chuck had set his sights on Hannah.

In an effort to distract his thoughts from the fact that he still had no evidence in Hannah's case, he pulled the file of last week's traffic citations and tried to concentrate on the report, but it was no good. All he could think about was Chuck's lesson that he'd witnessed and how well the Texan had played a role as a beginner in the sport of mounted archery. Ben clenched his fists as he recalled the way Chuck had smiled and flirted with Hannah and how she had been oblivious to what he was doing.

Ben hadn't been oblivious, though. At the time he had nothing other than a gut feeling that something wasn't right about the man. He'd tried to convince himself that it was just jealousy at seeing a man flirt with Hannah, but he'd had a feeling it was more. And he'd been right.

If he was truthful though, he'd admit that he *was*

jealous. He wanted her smiles reserved for him, but he hadn't been able to tell her that yet. In fact, he couldn't even respond when she'd tried to get him to open up about his feelings this morning. He might never be able to, and that scared him.

She'd looked determined when she told him that after this case was over he had to decide what he wanted. The problem was that he *knew* what he wanted, but he didn't know if he had the courage to reach out and grab it. He'd spent too many years telling himself that Laura's death had made him unworthy of ever being loved by another woman, and he wasn't sure he could overcome that feeling.

A knock on the door pulled him from his thoughts. "Come in."

The door opened, and Luke walked in. "Clara told me you wanted to see me. What do you need?"

Ben closed the report he'd had open and nodded. "I talked with Chuck Murray's ex-wife last night, and she gave me some interesting information about him. I'm expecting him to come in any minute now. I thought you might like to sit in on the interview since you've been such a big part of the investigation."

"Yeah, I sure would. Is there anything I need to do?"

Ben shook his head. "No, I'll lead out. You can jump in any time you think something needs clarifying."

"Okay."

Luke started to say something else, but a knock sounded on the door. "Come in," Ben called out.

The door opened, and Chuck Murray stood there. He looked just the way he had the day he'd gone to Hannah's ranch for his *lesson.* He was dressed in jeans and a Western-styled shirt, but today he wore a jacket. The same bolo tie he'd had on before hung around his neck.

Chuck walked into the room, a wary expression on his face. "Sheriff Whitman, here I am. You wanted to see me?"

Ben cleared his throat and nodded. "Thank you for coming, Mr. Murray. I appreciate you taking the time to come talk to us." He pointed to Luke. "This is my chief deputy, Luke Conrad. He's going to sit in on our meeting. Won't you have a seat?"

Chuck reached out and shook hands with Luke. "Nice to meet you, Deputy."

"Same here," Luke said before he sat down.

Chuck eased into the other chair in front of Ben's desk, sat back and crossed his arms over his midriff. "Now what can I do for you, Sheriff?"

"First off I'd like for you to tell me where you were yesterday afternoon about four o'clock."

Chuck's forehead wrinkled. "Four o'clock? I was at home feeding my horses."

"Was anyone with you?"

"No, I only have two horses, so I don't need any help. I hope that changes when I can buy my own place. Why would you ask?"

Ben reached down to the floor beside his chair and pulled one of the arrows he'd retrieved from the practice course the day before and laid it on his desk. "Do you recognize this arrow?"

A puzzled look lined his face, as he leaned forward

to study the arrow. "That's one of mine." He looked up at Ben. "Where did you get it?"

"From Hannah Riley's practice course. Someone tried to murder her with it yesterday."

Chuck's face paled, and his eyes grew round. "Murdered? With one of my arrows? But who?"

Ben leaned back in his chair. "I was hoping you could tell me that."

Chuck's body tensed, and he grabbed the arms of his chair. "Surely you don't think I could have done that."

Ben shrugged. "You've admitted it's your arrow."

"Yes, but someone must have stolen it." He sat up straight and snapped his fingers. "I remember. The other day I was doing some target practice in the backyard, and I went inside to get some water. I had a stack of arrows lying there, but they were missing when I got back. Someone could have stolen them while I was gone."

"That's kind of hard to believe," Luke said.

Chuck swiveled in his seat and glared at him. "That's the only time I can think of when I left any unattended, unless somebody broke into my house."

"Have you noticed anything else missing from your house?" Ben asked.

"No, but that doesn't mean—"

Before he could finish his sentence, Ben interrupted him. "Where were you night before last?"

"I was at home."

"Can anyone vouch for that?"

Chuck sat up straighter and frowned. "No, I was alone," he yelled. He took a deep breath, waited a moment and then spoke in a calm voice. "I didn't have anything to do with any attack on Hannah. I think she's a very nice person. From what I saw of the ranch, I could tell she's doing really well with it. I admire anyone who's successful in business."

Ben stared at him for a moment, and he detected a slight tremor in Chuck's lips. "Yes, Hannah's a wonderful person. That's why we want to make sure nothing happens to her." He paused a moment. "Tell me, how did you come to contact Hannah about taking mounted archery lessons?"

Chuck's lips pulled into a grim line. "I told you before that I saw her ad in the newspaper. Since I'd recently become interested in the sport, I thought she could help me."

Ben sat back in his chair and rolled the pencil he held between his fingers. "And how recent has it been since you started in the sport?"

"Right before I left Texas, about three months ago."

Ben leaned forward, opened the traffic citation file he'd been looking at before Luke walked in and pretended to study it. He could see Chuck leaning forward in his chair as if he was trying to get a glimpse of what the sheriff was looking at. Ben slapped the folder closed and folded his hands on top of it.

"Are you sure it hasn't been longer than that? My information tells me that you've been working on your skills for over ten years."

Chuck's cheeks turned red, and the muscles in his neck tightened. "That's a bald-faced..."

Ben held up his hand to stop him. "Don't make it

worse on yourself by lying. I know how long you've been competing, I know you were friends with Shane Riley, Hannah's husband, and I know about your jail time." He leaned forward and glared at Chuck. "So I suggest you think carefully about the statement you make here today."

Chuck didn't move for a moment, then he exhaled and sagged in his chair. "Okay. I see that you know more about my background than I thought, but I promise you I didn't have anything to do with trying to hurt Hannah Riley."

"Then why did you come here and seek her out with some phony story about wanting to learn mounted archery?" A sudden thought struck him. "Do you have some kind of vendetta against Shane Riley that makes you want to hurt his family?"

Chuck opened his mouth and started to speak but stopped and glared at Ben. "I have no vendetta against anybody, and I didn't try to hurt Hannah. I came here to talk to you today of my own free will because you asked me to, but I know my rights. If you have sufficient evidence that links me to a crime, then I suggest you arrest me now or I'm leaving."

Ben sat back in his chair and tossed the pencil he still held on his desk. "You're not under arrest, Mr. Murray, so you may leave."

Chuck rose to his feet and straightened his jacket. "Thank you, Sheriff. I wish I could say it's been a pleasure, but it hasn't."

He turned and walked to the door, but Ben called out to him just as he put his hand on the knob to open it. "You're still a suspect in a crime, Mr. Murray. Don't leave town, or I'll come looking for you."

Chuck turned and glared at him. "I'm not going anywhere. You know where to find me if you need to."

"And stay away from Hannah Riley."

The glare on Chuck's face turned to a grin. "I don't think that's up to you, Sheriff. I'll see what Hannah has to say about that."

Ben rose to his feet, planted his fists on his desk and leaned forward. "I'm warning you, Murray. Stay away from her."

A cruel laugh rippled from Chuck's throat, and he shook his head as he pulled the door open and then sauntered into the hall as if he didn't have a care in the world. Luke and Ben both stood as they listened to his footsteps fading down the hall. Luke walked over and shut the door that had been left open.

"Can you believe that guy? He as much as told you that he wasn't going to stay away from Hannah. He thinks he has the upper hand, doesn't he?"

Ben nodded. "Yes. Whatever it is he wants from Hannah, he still hasn't given up on getting it. He's a classic con man. He appeared to be charming when he met Hannah and me, but he was quick to lash out when he thought I was accusing him of something. The sad thing is that right now all I have are suspicions and circumstantial evidence, nothing that I can take to the district attorney."

Luke sighed. "Well, I'll keep digging. He has to have made a mistake somewhere."

"Thanks, Luke," Ben said. "What do you have on your schedule today?"

"Nothing other than patrol. Do you need me to do something?"

"That big trial over at Sevierville is scheduled to start tomorrow. I have to testify, but I don't know when I'll be called. I'd like you to hang around the office for me."

"Sure. No problem. I have some paperwork I can catch up on."

"And do me a favor. Will you call Hannah off and on through the day? She and Faith are both at home, and I want to make sure they're safe."

"I'll be glad to," Luke said. "I'll see you when you get back."

Ben watched Luke leave his office, and then he walked to the window and stared outside. He had hoped his meeting with Chuck Murray would yield something that would help him, but it hadn't. He was no closer to finding Hannah's attacker.

He wanted this case closed before she left for Korea, but it was looking doubtful at this point. Maybe if the DNA would come back, he would have a suspect, but who knew how long that would take. At the moment he had no idea which way to turn.

He needed a break in this case, and he needed it now. Something had to give soon.

TEN

Hannah stared out the window at the setting sun and sighed. She was bored with her regular routine interrupted. Two days ago she'd promised Ben she would cancel her classes. Now she was thinking she shouldn't have done that. All of her students with the exception of Chuck Murray were local residents that she'd known for years. Surely they could be trusted, even if Chuck couldn't.

The thought of Chuck made her stomach queasy. How could he have come here and deceived her? He had known Shane, and he had known about her. Ben's explanation that he had come to the Smokies to target her made sense, and it frightened her.

The ringing of her cell phone pulled her from her thoughts. She frowned as she looked at the unknown number on caller ID. Hesitantly, she connected the call. "Hello."

"Hannah, this is Chuck Murray."

As if her thoughts had conjured up his call, a chill ran up her spine. Her hand holding the phone trembled. "Wh-What do you want, Chuck?"

"I know the sheriff has probably talked to you before now and told you about my past, but I wanted to call and give you my side of the story."

Hannah's nostrils flared, and she gripped the phone tighter. "And what side would that be? Do you want to explain why I was almost killed by your arrows? Or maybe you want to tell me how you knew my husband, and you saw his widow as an easy target."

"No, no," he said. His pleading voice grated on her nerves. She wondered how many women he'd used that same tone with before. "It wasn't that way at all. As for the arrows, I have no idea who used them—several of my arrows were stolen a few days before they were used against you. I will admit I knew Shane. He talked about you and the mountains so much that I wanted to see them for myself and find out if you were what he had made me believe. So I decided to pretend I needed lessons when all I really wanted was to get to know you."

Hannah chuckled and shook her head. "You don't really think I believe that, do you? If you wanted me to trust you, then you shouldn't have started by lying to me when we met. But it doesn't matter to me why you did what you did. Now I know what you are, and I don't want you near me or on my property again. Do you understand?"

"Hannah, please give me a chance. You'll find I'm not such a bad guy when you get to know me."

"I doubt your ex-wife thinks you're such a great guy, especially after you nearly killed her."

"That was a long time ago." Hannah could hear the

desperation in his voice. "I'm a changed person. Please give me a chance to show you."

"I'm sorry, Chuck. You have no more chances with me. Please don't call or come by here again. I don't wish to have anything to do with you."

"Have it your way," he growled. Hannah's eyes flared at the abrupt change in his attitude. The sudden aggression ignited a small spark of fear. "But you're making a big mistake."

Before she had time to respond, he had disconnected the call. The tone of his voice when he spoke that last sentence concerned her. It sounded like a threat. She slowly lowered the phone and stuck it back in her jeans pocket.

"What's the matter, Hannah?"

She looked up to see Valerie standing in the door. Her eyebrows were drawn into a frown, and her worried gaze flitted over Hannah's face.

"That was Chuck Murray on the phone," she told her.

Valerie took a step into the room. "The one Sheriff Whitman warned you about?"

"Yes."

"What did he want?"

Hannah gave a small laugh. "He wanted me to give him another chance to show me what a great guy he is."

Valerie rushed over and grabbed Hannah's hand. "Tell me you didn't agree to that."

She shook her head. "No, but he ended the conversation by telling me I was making a big mistake. He made it sound like a threat."

"Then you have to call the sheriff right away and tell him. He needs to know this."

"I will." She looked past Valerie's shoulder and frowned. "Where's Faith?"

"She's in her room playing until dinnertime. Maria sent me to tell you that we'll be ready to eat in about an hour."

Hannah glanced down at her watch. "Tell Maria I'll be in to help her in a few minutes, but I want to talk to Ben first."

She waited until Valerie had left the room and then pulled her cell phone out and punched in Ben's number. It went straight to voice mail.

Hannah frowned. That was the second time today her call to Ben had gone to voice mail, and he hadn't responded to her earlier one, either. He had come by yesterday after work but had begged off on staying for dinner, saying that he was tired and just wanted to go home. The trial that had occupied most of his week had appeared to drain him of energy. That concerned her, but she'd always known his job was very stressful. And he had been scheduled to be back in court today.

When the phone beeped, she started her message. "Ben, this is Hannah. I wanted to tell you that Chuck Murray called me to apologize. He wanted me to give him another chance to get to know who he really is. I told him not to call me again. He wasn't happy to hear it, and at the end of the conversation, his tone got a little threatening. I thought you would want to know. Call me when you get a chance."

When she finished the message, she disconnected

the call and stood staring down at the phone in her hand. Guilt welled up in her, and she frowned. If she was honest with herself, she would admit that it wasn't only the trial Ben was involved in that was causing him stress. It was her situation also. What if it had all become too much for him and he was sick? The thought of his being ill made her stomach roil. She had to know if he was all right.

On impulse she punched in the number for Ben's office and waited for Clara to answer. "Sheriff's office."

"Clara, this is Hannah Riley. I haven't been able to reach Ben today. I wanted to check and see if you've heard from him."

"He just got back from court. I told him he looked like he was about to fall asleep on his feet and that he needed to take some time off. But of course he wouldn't listen to me. Hold on and I'll connect you to his office phone."

Before Hannah could object, Clara had transferred the call. Ben picked up right away. "This is Sheriff Whitman. How may I help you?"

"Ben, this is Hannah. I was worried because I hadn't heard from you today and wanted to see if you're all right."

He hesitated before he responded. "I was just listening to your voice mail. I'm sorry I missed your call. I just got back from Sevierville. I was still tied up in that trial all afternoon, but it was over today. Is everything okay with you and Faith?"

His voice sounded tired, and she could picture him rubbing his eyes. "Yes, we're fine."

"Good. I should be through around here in about thirty minutes. I'll run by and check on you then."

She started to agree, but then thought better of it. "You sound tired, and I know how you are when you get involved in a case. You won't eat. I'll tell Maria to prepare an early dinner, and you can eat with us. Then you need to go home and get some rest."

"I'm fine. I'll rest when the guy who's after you is caught."

"No, we're setting an extra plate at the table, and I won't take no for an answer."

He gave a slight chuckle. "I know how determined you can be when you make up your mind, so I'll just say that I'll see you later. Bye."

"See you later," she said and then disconnected the call.

Talking with Ben had only made her more concerned for him. He had enough on his mind with all the other problems in the county without having to babysit her. He'd been at her house over and over again when he wasn't on duty. Maybe she'd expected too much of him over the past few days. And then on top of that he might be experiencing stress because of the way she'd given him an ultimatum about what they should do about their personal relationship when her assailant was caught.

Her cheeks burned at the memory of what she'd said. But she had meant it. They needed to quit dancing around the question of what their feelings were for each other and come to an understanding. She couldn't live in the past anymore. She wanted a future for her and

Faith, and if it wasn't meant for her and Ben to share it, then she had to start looking for it somewhere else.

With that thought in mind, she went to help Maria with dinner.

Two hours later she and Ben sat in the den alone. Maria had shooed them from the kitchen the minute dinner was over with the command that everyone should get out so she could clean the kitchen. Valerie was upstairs helping Faith get ready for bed, and she and Ben were finishing their coffee.

Ben set his cup on the coffee table, sighed and laid his head back on the couch cushions. His eyes drifted closed for a moment, and then he sat up with a start. "I'm sorry. I almost dropped off to sleep."

Hannah smiled. "I hope it's not because the company is so boring."

He laughed. "You could never be boring. It's just been a busy week."

Hannah swiveled so that she was facing him. "And my problems have just added to it. I'm sorry. I don't want to add to the stress you already have in your job."

"You haven't. It's not your fault that some crazy guy has tried to kill you. No matter what else I have to do, I want you to know that I'll always be there for you."

She reached over and laid her hand on top of his. "And I will be for you, too."

He stared down at their hands for a moment before he raised his head and looked into her eyes. "Hannah, I've been thinking about what you said the other night."

"I hope you know I wasn't intending to put any pressure on you. It's just that I've put my life on hold for so long that I'm ready to live again. I want the future to be happy for Faith and me, so I have to decide how I'm going to go about doing that."

He nodded. "I thought you were happy with Shane. That's why it was such a shock when you told me what your marriage was really like. I can see how that experience would make you scared about putting yourself open to more hurt. And the last thing in the world I want to do is hurt you."

"You would never hurt me, Ben."

He shook his head. "You don't know that. Maybe you'd understand if I told you why I'm so afraid of commitment." He swallowed, and the sad look on his face made her heart pound in dread of what he was going to say. "I was in love once before when I was in college."

"You hinted at that once, but you've never told me the whole story."

"I know. It didn't end well, and it was all my fault." He hesitated, but when she didn't say anything, he spoke again. "I had strayed from the lifestyle that I'd been raised in. My parents were Christians, and I was brought up to know right from wrong. When I went away to school, though, I felt like I'd been set free to do anything I wanted, and I did. Drugs and alcohol took over my life to the point that my grades dropped, and I was put on probation by the university."

Hannah squeezed his hand. "But you graduated, didn't you?"

He nodded. "Later, I did—after I had gotten my life back together. But it took a horrible accident to make me wake up and see how I was wasting my life." He licked his lips and stared off into space as if she wasn't there. "Laura, the girl I loved, stuck by me and kept trying to help me, but I resented what I thought was her interference in my lifestyle. One night I took her to a party, and I got wasted. When we left, I was in no condition to drive, so she did. It was raining very heavily—visibility was poor and the roads were slick. The car skidded and hit a tree. I walked away without a scratch. Laura was killed."

Hannah blinked back tears and scooted closer to him. "I'm so sorry, Ben. I had no idea."

"After I got my life back together, I saw how my actions had affected someone I loved, and I knew I couldn't let it happen again. I decided that the best way to do that was to stay free of any commitments to another person. Be friends, don't get involved in a romantic relationship. Keep it light, because I don't want to fail another woman like I did Laura."

Hannah thought for a moment before she spoke. "I can see how that would affect you, but you're a different man now. You can't let what happened in the past take away any chance of happiness you may find with someone else. Don't you want to be happy?"

His eyes darkened, and he reached up and trailed his finger down her cheek. "I want to be, but I know I don't deserve it. I took Laura's life. I can't move on and make a good life for myself at her expense. Her memory will always be there, and it will remind me that I will fail someone else."

"Ben, you can't think that way. God wants all His

children to be happy. He would want you to forgive yourself and find peace and happiness."

He exhaled a deep breath. "I don't think I'll ever be able to do that. I've agonized over this for years, and I've prayed for forgiveness. I know God's forgiven me for my past, and He's blessed me greatly. The problem is I can't forgive myself."

She inhaled and closed her eyes for a moment. "After Shane died, I blamed myself for his unfaithfulness. If I had been prettier, if I had made him feel more important, if I had given him more money, he might have loved me enough to be faithful to me. I convinced myself that his cheating was all my fault. It took me a long time to realize that while I hadn't been a perfect wife, Shane was responsible for his own actions. When I came to see that, I asked God to forgive me. He did, and then He gave me two Bible verses that helped me so much."

"What are they?"

"They're found in Philippians—'this one thing I do, forgetting those things which are behind, and reaching forth unto those things which are before, I press toward the mark for the prize of the high calling of God in Christ Jesus.' So I came to know that I couldn't undo the past. I had to forget the past and live for the future. I want that for you, too."

He shook his head. "I don't know whether I can do that."

She released his hand, sat back on the couch and stared at him. "You know, Ben, we aren't promised tomorrow. I found that out when I thought that man was going to kill me. So I've decided I'm going to put my fears aside and live my life unafraid of what mistakes I may make tomorrow. I know whatever happens, God is going to be there with me, and I won't be facing each day without Him. All I can do for you is pray that God can open your eyes to do the same thing."

He bit down on his lip and nodded, then glanced down at his watch. "Thank you, Hannah. Now I think I'd better get on home. I have a busy day tomorrow. Turn your security system on and have a good night."

She rose to walk him to the door, but he was already closing it behind him before she could get out of the den. She listened as his truck started and drove down the driveway to the road. Obeying his instructions, she turned on the alarm. Only then did she turn toward the upstairs.

The conversation with Ben had been troubling, and she feared that the friendship she'd enjoyed with him through the years might be coming to a halt soon. She didn't think she could go back to the way they'd been, and he didn't seem to want to go forward.

For now, though, regular nighttime duties had to be taken care of. This problem was something she'd think about later after Faith was in bed and when she read her bedtime devotional.

Three hours later, Hannah was still worrying about her conversation with Ben when she crawled into bed. Her body ached, and she felt bone-tired, which surprised her. She knew what caused her to feel that way. Her talk with Ben. She stared up at the ceiling, pulled the covers up under her chin and sent a silent prayer to God that Ben could find a way to forgive himself. Her eyelids drooped as she lay there, and then she nodded off.

Sometime later the blare of the security system accompanied by a shrill scream shattered the quiet, and she bolted upright in bed. She glanced at the clock on the bedside table and saw that it was 2:00 a.m. The alarm roared through the house, and the scream came again. She jumped from the bed and dashed downstairs.

She'd just rounded the end of the staircase and turned toward the kitchen when a hysterical Valerie collided with her. The impact jarred both of them, and Valerie let out another squeal before she wrapped her arms around Hannah and held on tight.

"Valerie, what's wrong?"

The nanny jerked away from Hannah. In the dark hallway she couldn't make out Valerie's face, but she could feel her body shaking with sobs.

"Call the police," Valerie shrieked. "There's a man trying to get in the back door."

Ben had just drifted into a fitful sleep when his cell phone rang. He reached for it on the nightstand beside his bed and rubbed his eyes. "Hello."

"Ben, this is Luke. I thought you'd want to know. I'm on my way to Hannah's house. Her alarm system has been triggered."

Ben was out of bed and reaching for his clothes before Luke could finish what he was saying. "What happened?"

"Someone tried to break in the back door."

"Did he get inside the house?"

"No, the alarm went off, but evidently Valerie had gone into the kitchen, and she saw him. She's pretty shaken up."

"Are you sure everyone is okay?" By this time he was dressed and heading out the door.

"Yes, they're all fine."

"Where are you now?"

"I'm about two or three minutes away from her house. The deputies who responded first are already there."

"I'm on my way, too."

Ben ran out the front door of his house, jumped in his truck and roared out of the driveway on his way to Hannah's.

Ten minutes later he pulled into the front yard of Hannah's house. Luke's car and another squad car sat in the driveway. He was out of the truck and bounding up the front steps almost before the truck had come to a full stop. He ran through the front door. Luke met him in the entry.

"She's in the den."

He rushed through the doorway and stopped just inside the room. Hannah, clutching her hands in her lap, sat on the couch. She glanced up at Ben's entrance, and as soon as she saw him, her face crumpled. Tears ran down her cheeks as she jumped to her feet and ran to him. He opened his arms and wrapped her in them. For a moment all he wanted to do was hold her and assure himself that she was all right.

He turned his lips to her hairline right above her ear and gave her a soft kiss. At his touch, her body shook more, and she tightened her arms around his waist. "It's okay," he whispered. "I'm here now."

He rocked her back and forth for a few minutes before her sobbing quieted, and she pulled away from him. "I'm so glad you're here, Ben."

He glanced around the room. "Where is Faith?"

"The alarm system scared her. Valerie is upstairs with her now trying to get her back to sleep."

Ben led her back to the sofa and eased her down, then took a seat next to her. "Tell me what happened."

Hannah gave a little hiccup and wiped at her eyes. "Valerie said she couldn't sleep and thought she'd go to the kitchen and make some cocoa. When she was about to turn the light on, she saw something moving through the glass of the back door. The sound of the alarm and Valerie's screams woke me, and I ran downstairs," Hannah said.

"Could she tell if it was a man or a woman?"

"She thought it was a man."

"Did he break the glass?"

"No."

Ben was about to ask another question when Luke appeared in the doorway. "Ben, could I see you a minute?"

He stood and gave Hannah's hand a squeeze. "I'll be right back."

With his fists clenched at his sides, he stepped in the hall. "Tell me you've got something."

Luke glanced in the den and drew Ben a bit farther

away from the door as if he didn't want Hannah to hear. "One of the deputies found something on the ground outside the back door. I put it in an evidence bag."

Ben's heart skipped a beat. "What was it?"

Luke held up a plastic bag. "This."

Ben's eyes grew large, and his mouth opened wide. A bolo tie with a turquoise clasp lay curled inside the bag. He reached for the bag, held it up and examined it, and then smiled at Luke.

"That's Chuck Murray's tie. I think we should pay Mr. Murray a visit and see if he has an alibi this time."

ELEVEN

Hannah was still sitting at the kitchen table drinking a cup of coffee the next morning when Ben came in. His bloodshot eyes and his drooping shoulders told her that he hadn't slept the night before. She was on her feet and pouring him a cup of coffee before he was settled at the table.

She set it in front of him. His dark hair tumbled across his forehead, and he was still wearing the same clothes he'd had on when he'd rushed to her house last night. She swallowed hard to try to dispel the lump in her throat at how exhausted he looked. Without thinking, she reached out and smoothed his hair back from his forehead. To her surprise he seemed to lean into her touch as he closed his eyes and exhaled.

"Have you had breakfast?" she asked.

He shook his head. "No. I've been at the station all night. I wanted to come by and tell you that we arrested Chuck Murray. I've been questioning him for hours. He doesn't have an alibi, but he refuses to admit that he tried to break into your house last night."

"I'm going to fix you something to eat." She walked over to the refrigerator and pulled out bacon and eggs, then walked back to the stove and placed several slices of bacon in a frying pan. As it began to sizzle, she sat back down and crossed her arms on the table. She didn't say anything as Ben took another sip of coffee.

He ran his finger over the handle of the cup and frowned. "I couldn't get him to budge from his statement that he hadn't been anywhere near your house."

"Then how did he explain his tie being found here? Or did he claim it wasn't his?"

"When we showed it to him, he admitted that it looked like his. But then he said he hadn't worn it in days, and that somebody must have stolen it just like they did the arrows."

"What happens now?"

"We've booked him on suspicion of breaking and entering. I'm not sure we'll be able to make an attempted murder charge stick, though. I have a search warrant for his house, and I'm meeting Luke and two more deputies there in about thirty minutes. Maybe we can find something else that will link him to the case."

Hannah nodded but didn't say anything as she rose to finish cooking Ben's breakfast. Within minutes she set a plate filled with bacon, eggs and toast in front of him and refilled his coffee cup. He smiled and inhaled. "This smells so good, and I'm starved."

Hannah picked up her coffee and sipped as Ben began to devour his breakfast. Somehow it felt so right to be sitting here with him enjoying a morning cup of coffee. He glanced up, and their eyes met. He swallowed and set his fork down on his plate. Her skin tingled as his gaze drifted over her.

"This is nice being here with you," he said, his voice husky.

"I was just thinking the same thing," she whispered.

After a moment he picked up his fork and continued eating. A comfortable silence engulfed them, and a peaceful feeling bubbled up inside her. It suddenly dawned on her that she was in love with Ben Whitman. She didn't know when it had happened, but the friendship she felt for him had probably been turning to love for a long time. She wanted him in her life—wanted to build a future with him. But the question remained whether he would let her into his heart.

She had told him they couldn't return to what they'd been before, and now she was more convinced than ever. However, she didn't know if he would be able to put his past behind him and move on. If he couldn't, it would hurt, but she would survive. She just had to keep telling herself that.

Several hours later Ben, wearing latex gloves, sat in Chuck Murray's home office at his desk and sifted through the papers in all the drawers. He and his deputies had been busy for the last hour searching Chuck's house, but so far they hadn't found anything concrete that would connect Chuck to the attacks on Hannah. They had found his supply of arrows, matching the ones at the scene of Hannah's attack, but that link wasn't enough to take to the district attorney.

He picked up a piece of paper at the bottom of the

drawer he was searching and frowned. It was a receipt for a cell phone from a mall kiosk over at Knoxville. Something about the sale seemed strange to Ben. He remembered Chuck Murray's phone in his personal effects when he was booked last night, but he thought its number had a Texas area code. This receipt listed a Tennessee area code.

"Luke," he called out.

The deputy stuck his head in the doorway. "Yes?"

"Has anybody found a cell phone?"

Luke shook his head. "I don't think so. Why?"

"I just found the receipt for one that seems to be different from the one he had on him when he was arrested. Let me know if you come across one."

"Will do," Luke said. He started to step back into the hall but then stopped. "Oh, by the way. I called the local animal shelter about Murray's horses. They're going to send someone from the Smoky Mountain Equine Rescue Center out to get them. They keep horses of incarcerated people on a temporary basis until their court problems are resolved. Then they're either returned to the owner or put up for adoption."

Ben nodded. "Good. I'm glad they'll be taken care of. Are there any more animals?"

"A dog. I've called the Humane Society about him, and they should be here any minute to get him. They have the same policy as the equine center."

"Thanks for taking care of that, Luke."

Ben returned to his task of going through the desk drawers and had just closed the last one when one of his deputies walked into the room. He held a cell phone in his gloved hand. "Luke said you were asking about a cell phone. I found this one."

Ben stared at it a moment before he reached for it. He punched in his cell phone number and looked at the caller ID as the phone rang. It showed the same Tennessee number that had been on the receipt. This had to be the phone that had been purchased at the Knoxville mall.

He checked the texts, and he almost gasped aloud when the messages with the pictures of Faith that had been sent to Hannah showed up. He opened the photo app, and his heart dropped to the pit of his stomach as he stared at picture after picture of Hannah and Faith. Some were made at their house, some at Faith's school and others that appeared to be at spots around town.

He looked up at the deputy. "Where did you find this?"

"In a closet in Murray's bedroom. It was in a shoebox on the shelf."

Ben pulled an evidence bag from his pocket and dropped the phone in it. He didn't think Murray could explain away this evidence. With a record of his stalking Hannah and her daughter, combined with the arrows and the tie found outside Hannah's back door, he might finally have enough evidence to determine the charges sent to a grand jury.

He needed to talk to Chuck Murray, and he needed to do it now.

He jumped up from the desk and strode toward the front door. "Luke!" he yelled. "I'm on my way back to the office. Keep looking and see what else you can find."

As Ben drove toward his office, his anger got stronger and stronger. The one responsible for Hannah's attacks had been under his nose all along. He should have investigated the man further right after the first time he saw him, but he didn't want Hannah to think he was harassing an innocent person.

By the time he got to his office, his anger had risen to an explosion level. He barreled through the front door, gave Clara a curt nod and headed through the doorway that led to the cell block built onto the back of the building.

He stopped at Chuck's cell and glared at him. Chuck had been lying on the cot, and he slowly rose to his feet, walked to the cell's door and wrapped his hands around the bars. He stood there without saying a word and stared at Ben. The smug smirk from his last visit days before was long gone. Now he looked wary and uncertain.

Ben took a deep breath and held up the cell phone. "Do you know what this is, Mr. Murray?"

His eyebrows arched, and he didn't blink as he held Ben's stare. "Of course I know. It's a cell phone."

"You recognize it?"

Chuck studied it for a moment. "Can't say that I do."

"Then why was it found in a shoe box on the shelf in your bedroom?"

Chuck's eyes flared as if surprised. "I have no idea how it got there. It's not mine."

Ben shook his head. "I figured that's what you'd say. Just another coincidence like the arrows and the tie. Maybe a glance at some of the photographs on it will help jog your memory."

He held the phone back from the bars so that Chuck couldn't reach it as he began to scroll through the pictures. The muscle in his jaw flexed as Chuck couldn't seem to pull his gaze from the photographs.

When he'd finished, Chuck looked at him, fear in his eyes. "You've got to believe me, Sheriff Whitman. That's not my phone, and I didn't take those pictures."

For a moment Ben almost believed him, but then he remembered what the man's ex-wife had said, and shook his head. "Anybody hearing you now would believe you are innocent, but I know how con men play their games. They can make you believe whatever they want. So don't waste your breath trying to convince me. You'd better find yourself a lawyer and decide if you can make a jury believe you. I have a feeling the district attorney will think this is the evidence they need to charge you with attempted murder."

He turned and started to leave, but Chuck called out to him. "Sheriff, wait."

Ben turned back. "What is it?"

The muscles in Chuck's neck constricted, and he swallowed. "What about my animals? I have two horses and a dog. I'm worried about them. I don't know anybody here who can take care of them."

"That's been taken care of. They're in shelters and will be well cared for as long as you're in jail."

Relief flooded Chuck's face. "Thank you. I wouldn't want them to be hungry."

"Neither would I."

Having said that, he turned and walked out of the cell block. He felt conflicted after talking with Chuck Murray. The evidence against him was growing, and right now he was the chief suspect. But his concern over his animals painted a different picture of the man. Would someone who worried about the health and safety of animals in his care really threaten a small child?

Ben sighed as he walked to the evidence room to check in the phone. He tried to shake his doubts from his head. Even the worst of criminals could love their animals. That didn't cancel out the evidence. No, he wanted to believe they had the right man in custody, and he pushed aside the nagging sense of doubt. He needed to get back out to Chuck's home and help finish up the search. Maybe they'd find something else, but if they didn't, at least he already had some good news for Hannah.

Hannah laid the bridle she'd been cleaning on the table and stared around the tack room. It had been one of the best days Hannah had experienced in a long time. She had spent most of it helping Dusty in her favorite place, the barn. She loved everything about the place—the sounds of the animals mixed with the smells of hay, leather and even manure. She'd followed her grandfather through this barn when she was a little girl, and she still felt close to him when she was here.

Today was special, though. The burden of fear had lifted from her shoulders when Ben called to tell her about the cell phone they'd discovered. It was the clearest piece of evidence they'd found, and he'd said it should be enough to send Chuck Murray to trial.

In addition to her work in the barn today, she had even had time for a few hours of target practice. Maybe now Ben would agree to letting her go back to the practice course. She had a lot to make up for before she left for Korea.

She picked up the bridle again and hung it on a hook on the wall. With one last glance around, she walked out of the room and down the barn's alleyway. Just as she emerged outside, she heard the rumble of a truck, and she smiled as Ben drove around the side of the house and stopped beside the corral.

She stuck her hands in her jeans pockets and studied him as he climbed from the truck. Even though she knew he had to be tired, he walked today with a bounce in his step. He smiled as he stopped in front of her.

"I think it's over, Hannah. The district attorney is bringing charges against Murray for attempted murder."

Her breath left her, and she sagged. Ben caught her shoulders, and she smiled up at him. "Thank you, Ben."

A tear rolled from her eye, and he rubbed it away with his thumb. "I was just doing my job, but I have to admit this time it was more personal than ever before." He glanced over his shoulder. "Where is Faith?"

Hannah gave a short laugh. "She's at the house going through all her new clothes."

"Oh, did the GPS outfits come today?"

"They did, and she loves them. I've been working at the barn, but she's called me at least five times to tell me about how she loves the one she happens to be trying on at the time. Now we probably don't need them."

Ben shook his head. "Don't put them away. Until we know for sure that Chuck Murray is guilty, and confirm whether he had any accomplices, we're not taking any chances."

His words erased the relief she'd felt earlier, and she swallowed. "Do you think we might still be in danger?"

"I'm not saying that. I just think it's better to be safe than sorry. Besides you're leaving for Korea in a week, and you'll be going through some busy airports. It would be smart for her to wear them as a safety measure."

"I guess you're right," she said. "I put the app on my phone to track the GPS. Do you want it on yours?"

"I certainly do. Get in the truck, and I'll drive us back to the house so we can do that."

A few minutes later they walked into the house, and Hannah led him to the den where they downloaded the app. When he put his phone back in his pocket, Hannah stepped closer to him. "Do you really think Chuck Murray could be innocent?"

"I don't know, Hannah. All I can do is find the evidence and turn it over to the district attorney. It's his decision to pursue the case the way he wants. We still have the DNA out being tested. When that comes back, if it matches Murray's, then we'll have an open and shut case."

"When do you think it will be back?"

"I have no idea, but I don't want you to worry about this. You have a trip to plan. Concentrate on that."

"Is it okay for me to go back to the practice course?"

He hesitated for a moment. "I think so. Just be careful." He glanced at his watch. "Now I need to go. I need to see someone before I go home."

He turned to leave, but Hannah reached out and caught his arm. "Ben, are you still going with me to Korea?"

He looked at her, a surprised expression on his face. "I told you I would. What makes you think I'd change my mind?"

She didn't know if she could say what she was feeling, so she took a deep breath for courage. "I've thought a lot about that last talk we had about what our future might be, and I don't want you upset with me for anything I said."

His gaze softened, and he reached up and wrapped his fingers around a strand of her hair. "I could never be upset with you, Hannah." His voice sounded rusty, more like a growl. "You are the most important person in the world to me, and I want to be the kind of man you can depend on."

"You *are* that kind of man, Ben. I want you to see that."

His hand slipped to her nape, and he pulled her closer. "I don't want to fail you," he whispered.

"You could never do that," she answered.

His lips came closer, and she closed her eyes in anticipation of his kiss. She could feel his breath on her lips, then suddenly it vanished. She opened her eyes, and he backed away from her.

"I'll call you later."

Before she could object, he turned and walked from the room, leaving her feeling empty and alone.

Ben pulled to a stop in front of the barn at Dean's Little Pigeon Ranch and sat there for a moment thinking about what had happened with Hannah. He had wanted to kiss her so badly, and then at the last second he'd pulled away. He couldn't go on like this much longer, constantly torn about what to do. He needed to talk to someone, and the only person he wanted to confide in was his best friend, Dean.

He took a deep breath and crawled from the truck. He'd driven straight to the barn because he assumed that's where Dean would be at this time of day. He walked into the barn and straight to the tack room. Sure enough, Dean was inside.

He turned as Ben walked in. "Ben? I didn't expect to see you today. I heard you'd arrested a suspect in Hannah's case. I figured you'd be celebrating."

Ben shook his head. "I don't feel like celebrating. We did arrest a suspect, but I'm not sure the evidence will hold up."

Dean tilted his head to one side and frowned. "As a former lawman, I know all we can do is find the evidence and turn it over to the prosecutors. After that it's out of our hands."

Ben sighed. "Yeah, but my whole life seems to be out of my hands right now. That's why I came by. I need to talk to somebody."

Dean motioned to the chairs that sat beside a desk

in the corner. "Let's have a seat, and you can tell me all about it."

They settled in the chairs, and Ben clasped his hands in front of him. He sat there a minute staring down at them before he took a deep breath. "It's Hannah."

Dean didn't move for a moment, and then he leaned forward. "What about Hannah?"

"I'm in love with her, Dean."

A big grin pulled at Dean's face. "I've known that for years, Ben. I've seen the way you look at her and how protective you are of her. What's the problem? Doesn't she feel the same way?"

"I think she does. At least, she's told me that she doesn't want us to continue our friendship the way it is now—she'd like to take it further, see where it could go. She wants to move on with her life and make a future for her and Faith. And I don't blame her for that. I just don't know if I can move on with her."

"Because of Laura?"

Ben jerked his head up and stared at Dean. "You know how hard it's been for me to live with that guilt."

Dean sighed. "I know, but Ben, you can't let it control your life forever. God wants you to be happy, and He's given you a wonderful woman who could share a great life with you, not to mention a beautiful little girl who I know you adore. Don't lose this opportunity to have the blessings He's sent you."

Ben sat silent for a moment. "I just don't want to hurt Hannah or Faith. I would give my life for either one of them."

Dean scooted to the edge of his chair. "You are the best friend I have, and you're the kindest man I've ever encountered. You are so quick to forgive what others do to you, but for some reason you can't forgive yourself."

"That's what Hannah said. She even quoted a Bible verse to me about putting the past behind you and looking to the future."

"And she's right. I've told you that for years. Now Hannah's told you also, but we can't do it for you. You're going to have to decide if hanging on to that guilt is worth losing Hannah and Faith in your life. To me it's a no-brainer to choose them, but I can't make you do it. But I will pray that you make the right decision."

"Thanks, Dean. I'll pray, too."

Dean stood. "Just don't wait too long. Gwen and I almost lost out on our happiness because of stubbornness on both our parts, and you were the one who pointed me in the right direction. I want to do that for you."

Ben rose from his chair. "Thanks, Dean. I'm going with Hannah to Korea for a competition, but I'll talk to you before then."

"You do that."

They walked from the barn, and Ben climbed in his truck. The sun was just beginning to go down, and he stared at it setting over the mountains back of the ranch. He closed his eyes for a moment. "Help me, God. I love her so much, but I've told myself for years I didn't deserve to have someone else love me. Show me what to do. Should I tell her how I feel, or should I walk away?"

He sat still for a moment, but there was no answer. Finally, he started the truck and drove from the ranch.

TWELVE

A week later, Hannah stood in her bedroom thinking about how peaceful her life had been since Chuck was put in jail. Life had returned to normal at the ranch, and now the day had finally arrived that she was to leave for Korea. When she'd first considered entering the competition, it had seemed like an adventure that was far in the future, but now it was upon her. In a few hours she would be on her way. It was the first step toward the new life she wanted.

No longer was she going to let all the demeaning and verbally abusive remarks Shane had hurled at her during their marriage affect her. She was going to embrace her abilities, and she was going to step out unafraid to try new things.

The one troubling thought that plagued her, however, was whether Ben was going to be a part of her future. She had prayed about their situation, but so far she hadn't received any sign that her prayers had been answered. Maybe this was God's way of telling her they weren't meant for a relationship beyond friendship. She would have to accept it if that was correct. It would be difficult, but just like she had told Ben, she would forget the past and look to the future.

He was still going with her to Korea, and she was happy about that. At least they could enjoy spending time together away from the mountains and in a different culture. She had been reading about all the places to visit near where the competition was being held, and she already had all their free time booked with excursions.

She looked at the suitcase on her bed and checked to see if she'd put in everything she would need. Then she walked to Faith's room and smiled as she drew near. She could hear Faith and Valerie talking excitedly about the things they were going to see in Korea. When she entered the bedroom, Valerie was just closing Faith's suitcase.

"It looks like you are about ready to go."

Valerie looked up and smiled. "We're all packed. I've already put my suitcase in the car. Do you want me to take the rest of them out?"

"If you'll take Faith's, I can get my own. I need to make sure Maria knows our itinerary and where we'll be staying."

"What about your horse? When is Dusty leaving with him?" Valerie asked.

"He left about thirty minutes ago with Blaze in the trailer. We'll meet up at the airport and make sure the horse gets settled properly. I'm afraid this isn't going to be a good experience for Blaze."

"I'm sure he'll be all right." Valerie pulled the suitcase off the bed and turned to Faith. "Let's go out through the kitchen so we can tell Maria goodbye."

"Okay," Faith said as she ran from the room.

Valerie started to follow her, but Hannah stopped her. "Valerie, I want to thank you for going on this trip with us. I can never thank you enough for what you've done for us since you've come to work here. Faith loves you, and I really appreciate how great you are with her."

Valerie's face flushed, and she smiled her shy smile. "Thank you, Hannah. I've loved being here. It's started to feel like home, and I'm excited about our trip."

"Me, too. Now go catch up with Faith, and I'll see you downstairs in a few minutes."

Hannah went back to her room, grabbed her suitcase and had just gotten downstairs with it when she heard a knock at the door. She opened it, and Ben stood there. Today he wasn't wearing his uniform. He was dressed comfortably for traveling in jeans and a crisp white shirt. He smiled when he saw her. "Ready to go?"

She nodded. "Just as soon as I get my suitcase in the car."

He reached for it. "Let me take this."

She handed the bag to him and turned toward the kitchen. "I want to check with Maria once more before I leave. Then I'll come on out."

She found Maria putting the breakfast dishes in the dishwasher. She turned when Hannah entered the room and wiped her hands on her apron. "So are you ready to go?"

"We are. I just wanted to check to see if you know where we'll be."

Maria laughed. "I think you've told me at least three times. I have it all written down, but don't you worry about us here. You go and have a good time, but we expect you to come home a winner."

"I don't know if I'll be able to do that or not, but I'll try." She gave Maria a quick hug. "Thank you for all you do for us."

When Maria released her, she stared at Hannah, a worried expression on her face. "Are you sure you should be going? I know that man is still in jail, but I saw that statement from his lawyer in the paper, saying he's denied having anything to do with the attacks against you. What if he's not guilty? I don't want you and Faith to be hurt."

Hannah reached out and squeezed Maria's hand. "I understand your concern, but nothing has happened since Chuck Murray was arrested. That tells me that he's responsible for the attacks. And Ben is going to be with us, so he'll see that we stay safe."

Maria bit down on her lip and nodded. "Well, then, have a good time."

"I will." Hannah hugged her one more time and ran out the door.

Faith and Valerie had already gotten in the back seat of the car, but Ben was leaning against the back fender. The trunk lid was open, and he straightened when she came out of the house. "I put the bags in the car, but I wanted to make sure you didn't have something else."

She shook her head. "No, that's it. I'm ready to go."

He stepped back and slammed the trunk lid down. "Then let's be off." He'd taken only a few steps toward the driver's door when his cell phone chimed. He pulled it from his pocket and frowned. "It's the office. What could they want? They know Luke is in charge until I get back."

"You'd better answer it," Hannah said, "or Clara will track you down."

He chuckled. "I suppose you're right." He connected the call. "Hello."

After a moment his eyebrows arched, and his face lit up. "Really? Thanks for calling. I'll be right there."

"What is it?" Hannah asked as he ended the call.

"That was Clara. She wanted me to know that the DNA results have come back."

Hannah's heart skipped a beat. "That's wonderful. Do they match Chuck Murray?"

"She didn't know. She thought I might want to look at them before we leave."

A frown pulled at Hannah's brow. "How long do you think you'll be? I need to get to the airport and see that Blaze is settled."

"It shouldn't take long," he answered. "But you take Valerie and Faith and go on. I'll go to the office and look at the results, then I'll catch up with you at the airport. I'll call you when I'm leaving the office."

"All right. We'll see you at the airport."

He started to leave but turned and faced her. "By the way, I saw the weather report this morning. We're expected to get some high winds today. Be careful.

You know our strong winds can cause a car to swerve on these mountain roads."

She smiled. "I'll be sure to keep both hands on the wheel."

He stared at her for a moment, and his eyes softened. "Do you realize this may be the end of the search for the person who's tried to kill you?"

"I do. Thank you for never giving up on finding him."

He reached out and cupped her face with his hand. "I almost gave up on something else, but I've begun to deal with that. I've done a lot of thinking and praying, and I can't walk away from you. I'm glad I'm going on this trip with you. I have lots to talk to you about while we're in Korea. I think it's time we discussed the future that I want us to share."

She blinked back tears. "Are you sure?"

He nodded. "I can't lose you, Hannah."

"I don't want to lose you either, Ben."

He brushed his lips across her cheek and then ran to his truck, which he'd intended to leave at her house. Hannah watched as Ben jumped in and drove from the driveway. Then she climbed in her car and started it.

Faith squirmed in her car seat. "Why is Ben not coming with us?"

She smiled, her heart lighter than it had been in years. "He had some business at the office, but don't worry. He'll meet us at the airport." She looked over her shoulder at Valerie and Faith in the back seat. "So is everybody buckled and ready for an adventure in Korea?"

"Yes!" Faith squealed. "Let's go, Mommy."

Hannah laughed and pulled out onto the road. As she drove away, she thought of what awaited her in Korea. She would be competing against the best mounted archers in the world. A year ago she would never have believed she would step out of her comfort zone like this, but now she had.

The world of mounted archery was small, and it wouldn't take long for word to get around that she was back. She could hardly wait to see what the future held for her.

She glanced over her shoulder and smiled at the sight of Valerie and Faith engrossed in one of the new books she had bought for Faith to enjoy on the trip. Maybe that would entertain Faith all the way to the Asheville airport.

Up ahead she spotted a sign that told her she'd reach the I-40 in one mile. A sudden gasp from the back seat caused her to jerk her head around. She frowned at the look of shock on Valerie's face. "What is it?" she demanded.

Valerie frowned and shook her head. "I just realized I left my medication for motion sickness at home. I'll need it on the plane." She pointed at a roadside market near the interstate. "Would you mind stopping so I can get some there?"

"Sure," she said as she guided the car into the store's parking lot. "I don't want you to get sick on the plane."

Valerie opened the door and stepped out. "Thanks, Hannah. I'll only be a moment."

She turned and ran into the store. Hannah swiveled

in her seat and smiled at her daughter. "Are you excited about the trip?"

Faith nodded. "Yes. But I wish Ben could have left with us."

"Don't you worry. He'll meet us at the airport. We're all going to have a grand time together."

The words were no sooner out of her mouth than the rear door opened. She looked up expecting to see Valerie. Instead, a man she'd never seen before slid into the back seat next to Faith. Fear rose in Hannah's throat. She'd never seen his face clearly before, but she knew right away who he was—the man who had attacked her three times.

She opened her mouth to speak, but he silenced her by exposing the gun he held in his hand. Hannah began to shake at the sight of the weapon pointed toward Faith. "Don't make any noise, or you'll be sorry," he growled.

Hannah looked around the parking lot, hoping to see someone who could help her, but there was no one there. At that moment, Valerie stepped out of the market and hurried toward the car. Hannah wanted to cry out to her to run, to get help, but fear of what the man might do to Faith had paralyzed her.

Valerie headed straight toward the car and opened the passenger door of the front seat. It took a moment for Hannah to realize she had gotten in the car next to her instead of returning to the back where she had sat before—the seat her attacker occupied now. Almost as if she knew he would be there.

Hannah frowned and shook her head in confusion. "What…"

Valerie smiled and glanced over her shoulder at the man in the back seat. "I told you it would be easy."

"V-Valerie," she stammered. "I don't understand. What's going on?"

Suddenly Valerie's face dissolved into a mask of disgust. She leaned toward Hannah and snarled, "You don't have to understand right now. Give me your cell phone, and just drive where I tell you to go."

Hannah looked over shoulder at Faith, whose eyes were wide with fear, and her heart pricked. She blinked back the tears pooling in her eyes and offered Faith a shaky smile. "Don't worry, darling. Everything's going to be fine. You just sit still until we get to wherever Valerie and her friend are taking us."

Hannah felt something nudge her ribs, and she looked down to see that Valerie had a gun pressed against her side. "Your cell phone?"

Reaching in her pocket, Hannah pulled out the phone and handed it to Valerie. "Now what do you want me to do?"

"Turn around and head back the way we came. I'll tell you when to turn."

Hannah took a deep breath and nodded. Then she started the car and got back onto the road, heading away from the airport. She had no idea where they were going, but for now she would do as she was told. She couldn't let anything happen to Faith.

Ben glanced at his watch as he pulled to a stop at his office. Maybe he should have gone on with Hannah, but he really wanted to see the DNA results. Hannah would enjoy the trip more if she knew they had the last piece of evidence that would confirm Chuck Murray as her attacker. There was still plenty of time to get to the airport and get checked in before the flight left.

He climbed from his truck and entered the building. Clara looked up from her desk as he came in the door. "I shouldn't have called. I hate that you came by here. Luke could have looked at the results and emailed you the information."

He shook his head. "No, I'd rather look at it myself. I'll need to let the district attorney know. Where's the report?"

"I put the results in a file folder. It's on your desk."

He cocked an eyebrow and grinned at her. "And you didn't take a peek to see what it said?"

She huffed out a breath and glared at him. "I'll have you know I don't stick my nose into official business. You've told me often enough I'm here to answer the phone and dispatch to the deputies."

"I'm glad to see you're taking your job seriously," he said as he tried to smother the smile pulling at his lips.

Clara lifted her chin and picked up some folders on her desk. "Besides, I received a call about a robbery, and I've been busy with the deputies ever since."

Ben didn't say anything but shook his head and laughed as he walked to his office. Once inside he settled in his desk chair and looked down at the manila folder in front of him. Finally, it had arrived with what he hoped would be the end of Hannah's nightmare.

Taking a deep breath, he opened the folder, picked up the papers inside and began to read. His heart plummeted to the pit of his stomach the longer he read. He couldn't believe what he was seeing. There was a DNA match to someone who had been in the prison system, but it wasn't Chuck Murray. The DNA belonged to a man named Wes Allen.

Ben sat back in his chair and blinked. Wes Allen? Who was this man? He'd never heard of him before.

After a minute he picked up the report again and continued to read. Wes Allen had served time in prison for assault but had been released recently. There was nothing about the crime in the report that gave him a clue to what his connection to Hannah could be. He scanned down the report for the name of the town where the crime had occurred. Laredo, Texas.

It took him only a minute to find the town's police station number, and he dialed it and asked to be transferred to the criminal investigation division. A male voice answered right away. "Detective Willis."

"Detective," Ben said, "my name's Ben Whitman, and I'm the sheriff of Sevier County, Tennessee. I've just got a DNA report back from a crime scene here. It's a match for a man who was convicted of assault in your jurisdiction and served some time. His name is Wes Allen. Do you remember anything about that case?"

"Wes Allen? Let me check my records here." Ben waited impatiently, but it took only a moment before Willis was back on the phone. "Yeah, I remember now. It was a case of two cowboys getting in an argument at a bar, and the other guy accused Wes of trying to kill him. Witnesses supported what the man said, and Allen ended up serving time for it."

Ben had been busy scribbling down everything the detective said. "Do you know who the guy was that was attacked?"

"Um-m-m, let me see here. Oh, yeah. His name was Shane Riley. Both these guys were in town for a mounted archery training workshop, and Allen tracked Riley to a bar. An argument broke out, and it ended up with Allen arrested."

Ben's stomach was doing flip-flops the longer the detective talked. "Do you know what the argument was about?"

"Allen was angry because Riley had been having an affair with his sister, and she became pregnant. When Riley refused to acknowledge that he was the father, the woman tried to commit suicide. She wasn't successful, but she had a miscarriage."

Ben's hand was shaking now. "What's the sister's name?"

"Julie Allen."

Ben searched his mind for someone by that name, but he couldn't place her. "Do you have any more information on her?"

"Well, she was with her brother at the bar that night, and witnesses said she attacked Riley, too. She was arrested, but she had to be released because her brother said she wasn't involved. He took total responsibility." He paused a minute. "I have a mug shot of her. Would you like for me to send it to you?"

"I'd appreciate that. And send Wes Allen's picture, too, please." Ben rattled off his email address.

"Will do," the detective replied.

"Thanks, Detective Willis. You've been a great help."

"Anytime."

Ben hung up and waited for the chime that an email had arrived. When it alerted him, he pulled up the first picture. It was a man he'd never seen, but he seemed to be about the same height and build as Chuck Murray.

Then he opened the second attachment, and cold fear rushed through his veins. The face staring back at him was from the woman he knew as Valerie Patrick, but apparently her real name was Julie Allen. For a moment all Ben could do was gape at the picture. The person responsible for Hannah's harrowing experiences had been close to her all along, disguised as a friend while she was plotting the murder of the woman whose husband had fathered her child.

Suddenly a new thought popped into his head, and he jumped to his feet. Hannah and Faith were on their way to the airport unaware that the person who wanted to harm them was in the car with them. He had to warn her before it was too late.

Ben pulled his cell phone from his pocket and punched in Hannah's number. It rang several times before it went to voice mail. "Hannah!" he yelled into the phone. "Get away from Valerie as quick as you can. She isn't who she says she is, and you and Faith are in danger."

He disconnected the call and tried again. It went to voice mail again. Maybe she couldn't get to her phone because she was driving, he thought, but then he reminded himself that she had Bluetooth. It would have come up on her car's system unless the phone was turned off, and Hannah never turned her phone off.

He raked his hand through his hair and groaned. Hannah and Faith were in trouble. He could feel it in every bone of his body. He had to find them, but he had no idea where to start.

He grabbed his gun from the desk drawer, where he'd intended to leave it while he was on the trip to Korea, and strapped it on. Then he turned and ran from his office.

THIRTEEN

Hannah had no idea where they were going, but she kept following Valerie's commands. They'd turned off the main road a few miles back, and now they were winding through a remote area where the road climbed up the mountain. From time to time she spotted a road that turned off to the left or right, but Valerie kept directing her to go straight.

She glanced over her shoulder at Faith, who was crouched in her car seat, her eyes riveted on the man beside her. "Valerie," Hannah whispered. "Why are you doing this? Did I do something to hurt you?"

The woman gave a sarcastic chuckle. "You could say that. If you'd given Shane a divorce like he'd wanted, I wouldn't be here."

Hannah's mouth dropped open, and she swerved to the side of the road. She quickly corrected the car and shook her head. "What are you talking about? Shane never asked me for a divorce."

"Don't give me that," Valerie snarled. "He told me how you laughed at him and refused to consider a divorce when he told you I was pregnant with his child."

"He never told me anything about you. Certainly not that he'd gotten anyone pregnant."

Valerie laughed. "Don't lie to me. He told me you said you'd never give him a divorce and that I deserved whatever I got for having an affair with a married man."

Hannah shook her head. "I never said that. I didn't know anything about you. I knew Shane was unfaithful, but that's because he wasn't very good at hiding it. He never talked to me about his affairs, never admitted that he was seeing other women."

"Do you really expect me to believe that? I was the one he turned to for comfort for all those months while he tried to make you give him the divorce, but he said you threatened to take Faith away and never let him see her again if he left you. That's when he told me he had to go back to you. I was so devastated that all I wanted to do was die. I tried to do that, but I only ended up killing my baby." She pushed the gun harder against Hannah. "You took away my baby, and the man I loved. Now I'm going to get my revenge."

Hannah gripped the steering wheel tighter. "Valerie, I promise you that I never knew anything about this."

"Not even when you told Shane to file charges for that fight they had in that bar?"

"What fight?"

"Don't act like you didn't know. My brother confronted him about what had happened to me, and they got into a fight. Shane wanted to pass it off as a friendly disagreement, but he said you insisted the only way to get us out of his life was to press charges. So he did, and my brother went to prison."

Hannah looked at the man in the back seat. "Is this your brother?"

Valerie nodded. "He's always taken care of me. When I tried to kill myself, he was free on bail, and he was so upset he decided to try to talk to Shane once more. He knew Shane was in Houston, so he followed him there and confronted him again. Shane got violent, and Wes killed him in self-defense." She sighed. "So you see how you've ruined our lives, all because you wouldn't let your husband go when he wanted to."

By this time Hannah was shaking so hard that it was difficult to hold the steering wheel. "Valerie..."

"My name is Julie," she interrupted. "Valerie Patrick is the name of a girl whose purse I stole in a mall and assumed her identity."

"So how did Chuck Murray fit into all this? Was he your accomplice?"

Julie laughed. "Of course not. We'd never seen him before, but he made the perfect scapegoat. It was so easy for Wes to take those arrows and his tie from his house and plant the phone there. Then Wes and I staged the attempted break-in so he could leave the tie outside where it would be sure to be noticed." She glanced over her shoulder and glared at her brother. "If he'd been a better shot at the practice course, this would have been over that day. But he wasn't. I've always told him he needs to practice more."

Hannah gritted her teeth. "You realize Sheriff Whitman won't let you get away with this."

"Ah, yes, the sheriff. We'd planned to shoot him in the parking lot and dump his body along the mountain road, but he got that call and had to go to the station. So he gets to live, I guess."

Hannah didn't say anything for a moment as she thought of the reason Ben had to go back to the station. Julie hadn't overheard their conversation, so she had no idea the DNA results had come in. Wes had a criminal record, so his DNA would be in the system. By this time Ben had to know the identity of the man who'd tried to kill her. She didn't know if that would help him find them or not, but she prayed it might. But even if it meant that the brother and sister were caught in the end, would it happen soon enough to keep her and Faith alive?

"You talk too much," Julie muttered. "Just drive."

Hannah glanced at Julie and sucked in her breath at the wild look in her eyes. How could she have been so fooled by her? The woman was obviously mentally ill, and her brother in the back seat was also unstable and aggressive as demonstrated by his attacks on her and his threats against Faith. She needed to stay calm and not upset them more. She also needed to assure Faith that they were going to be all right. That was going to be the hardest thing of all, because she had no idea if they were going to survive this.

As she had done the night Wes had abducted her at Bart's Stop and Shop, she breathed a prayer. *God, I don't know what's going to happen, but I pray for Your protection over my daughter. She's too young and innocent to be a victim of these two people. Help us, Lord.*

"Turn right up here." Julie interrupted her thoughts.

Hannah did as she said, and guided the car down a narrow lane that ended in the yard of a cabin about five hundred feet from the road. When the car came to a stop, Julie turned to her brother. "Take the kid inside first. Hannah won't give me any trouble if she thinks Faith's in danger."

"Please, no," Hannah said as she reached to open the door. She needed to get to her daughter.

Julie pressed the gun against her once again. "Be still, or you'll be sorry."

"Mommy!" Faith shrieked as Wes picked her up and carried her inside.

Hannah whirled in her seat to face Julie. "How can you be so cruel to a little girl? She's never done anything to you."

Julie shrugged. "It hurts to know your child's in danger, doesn't it? That's how I felt when I knew that mine had died, and it was all your fault."

"What can I say to make you believe I never knew anything about you?" Hannah yelled.

Julie studied her for a moment. "Nothing. Now get out of the car. We have business to take care of inside."

With a resigned sigh, Hannah opened the door and stepped out of the car. Her legs shook so hard that she thought she might collapse. She looked around at the trees surrounding the cabin. They were in the middle of a forest on a mountain in the Smokies, and no one knew where they were. Their situation felt hopeless, but she couldn't let Faith see her fear.

Lifting her chin and fisting her hands at her sides,

she marched toward the front door of the cabin like a prisoner headed toward his execution, and she feared that was exactly what was about to happen.

Ben ran past a surprised Clara and out the front door of the building to his truck. When he reached it, he stopped in frustration and banged his fist on the fender. He had no idea where to look for Hannah and Faith. His unanswered phone calls told him that his warning had come too late. Had Valerie or Julie or whatever her name was harmed them already, or had she taken them somewhere?

At that thought he straightened to his full height and groaned. Why hadn't he thought of it sooner? He'd told Hannah to dress Faith for the trip in one of the outfits that had the hidden GPS sewn into the garment. He yanked his phone from his pocket and opened the tracking app. A moving arrow on the screen pinpointed the area where the car was located.

He ran back into the office. "Clara!" he yelled.

"What?" she shrieked in terror.

"Get Luke on the phone. Tell him I need backup. Hannah and Faith are in trouble. They're headed into the mountains, and I'm going after them. Tell him I'll go in my squad car so that he can track me." Thankfully, all the squad cars were outfitted with GPS beacons.

Clara grabbed the phone, and he turned and ran from the building. His squad car sat at the curb, and he jumped in and roared from the parking lot. Now he had to follow the signal being given off by Faith's clothes, secure in the knowledge that Luke could track him.

He glanced at his cell phone again and frowned. The car had come to a stop. He had no idea what was at that location, but now he knew where they were. He only hoped he could get there in time to save them.

Inside the cabin Hannah huddled on a leather couch that had seen better days and tried to keep from frightening Faith who she hugged close to her body. For the last few minutes Julie and Wes had talked in low whispers across the room, and she'd been unable to hear what they were saying.

Wes hadn't talked much on their way here, but the sound of his voice was seared in her memory. She'd heard it before when he kidnapped her and held a gun on her. From where she sat now, she could tell that Julie was going over the plan of what he was to do. He glanced in her direction once in a while and then nodded to Julie. Whatever they were discussing, it didn't bode well for her and Faith.

After a few minutes Wes turned and walked out the door, leaving them alone with Julie. She walked over and sat down in a chair facing them. "Scared?" she asked.

Hannah wasn't about to let her think she was frightened. "Don't expect me to cower before you. I know there's no dealing with a crazy person, and you sure fit that description. Not only are you crazy, but you are also evil. Even if you refuse to budge from the idea that I'm somehow to blame for what happened, Faith did nothing to hurt you. What kind of person dreams up a story like the one you told me and uses it as an excuse to harm an innocent child?"

Julie's jaw clenched. "I didn't make up the story. Shane loved me, and he would have married me if it hadn't been for you and your brat."

Hannah shook her head and laughed. "Shane didn't love anybody but himself. Do you think you were the only woman he had an affair with? I lost count of how many there were years ago. He might have used me as an excuse to get rid of the clingy ones, but that's all it was—an excuse. If he had ever asked me for a divorce, I would have given it to him gladly just to be rid of him. You had nothing to fear from me."

Julie jumped to her feet. "You're lying! He loved me."

Hannah realized that it didn't matter what she said. Julie was never going to believe her. Suddenly she felt sorry for the woman who her husband had treated so badly. She'd always wondered if Shane's unfaithfulness had been her fault, but now she saw the truth. He had never been the decent, honorable man she'd thought she was marrying. He had used her and the money she gave him for his own selfish purposes and didn't care about her or Faith—or Julie, or any of the other women he'd used and abandoned over the years. He was nothing like Ben.

The thought of Ben made her stomach clench. What would he do when he got to the airport and found that they had never arrived? He would have no idea where to look for them. Her eyes filled with tears. Just an hour ago she'd been so happy when Ben told her they needed to talk about their future. Now it didn't look like they would have a chance to make that happen.

The front door opened, and she looked over to see Wes entering the cabin. Before he could close the door, a strong gust of wind caught it, jerked it from his hands and slammed it backward against the wall. He grabbed for it and pushed on the door to close it.

"The wind is getting really strong. We need to finish up here and get going."

The words *finish up here* sent cold chills down her spine. What were these two planning?

Julie nodded. "Is everything ready outside?"

"Yeah. The brush is stacked next to the cabin, and it's ready to go."

Those words washed over her, and Hannah hugged Faith closer. It sounded like Julie and Wes were planning to light the cabin on fire, with Faith and Hannah trapped inside. They were about to die, and it was going to be painful. *Oh, God. Help my daughter survive this. Take me if you must, but please leave her.*

"Have you got the rope?"

The question startled Hannah, and she cringed.

"It's right here." He walked over to a cupboard, opened the door and pulled out a coiled length of rope.

Hannah's heartbeat raced as he walked toward her. "What are you going to do?"

Wes inclined his head toward a chair that sat at a kitchen table. "Get in that chair and put your hands behind your back."

Hannah tightened her arms around Faith. "No."

Wes took two steps and towered over her, rage written on his face. Without speaking he reached down and wrenched Faith from her arms. Hannah screamed as Faith cried out and grabbed for her.

Julie stepped between them and smirked down at Hannah. "Cooperate or we can make it worse."

"Mommy! Mommy!" Faith screamed over and over.

Helpless, Hannah watched as Wes tied Faith to one of the chairs and then motioned for Hannah. "You next."

On trembling legs, Hannah rose and stumbled across the floor. All she wanted to do was comfort Faith, but Julie held her back from going to her daughter. With a strangled cry Hannah sank onto the chair and felt her body go cold all over as Wes tied her up.

When he'd finished, he stepped back and nodded to Julie. She moved in front of Hannah. "You are the reason for a lot of grief in my life and my brother's. We had to wait for revenge until Wes got out of jail, but now it's time. In a way, I'm actually glad that Wes wasn't able to kill you with those arrows on the practice course. Shooting you would be too quick, too easy. I want you to have time to think about how you brought this on yourself and your daughter as you die. Goodbye, Hannah."

With that they turned and walked out the door. She heard the key turn in the lock and knew she and Faith were alone now. Faith squirmed in her chair and turned to look at her mother. "Valerie is a bad person, isn't she?"

A lump formed in Hannah's throat. "Yes, darling. I'm afraid she is."

"Are you scared, Mommy?"

At the moment she was more scared than she'd ever been in her life. If only there was something she could do to save her child, but she was helpless. She cleared her throat to speak past the lump there.

"There's no need to be scared, darling. Haven't I always told you that God watches over you? He's going to take care of you."

Hannah couldn't tell her that God might have plans to take care of her soul once she left her body behind, so she didn't add to her statement.

Faith sighed. "I know, Mommy. I've been praying that God will send Ben to save us, and I know He will. You just wait and see."

"I hope you're right, darling."

Hannah started to say more, but she froze. Her eyes grew wide, and her nostrils twitched as the smell of smoke filtered into the room. She turned and stared toward the wall of the cabin and then heard a crackling sound.

Brush, Wes had said. He had placed brush against the cabin, and now it was on fire. They were trapped and were about to be consumed in an inferno. With a surge of energy, she strained at the ropes holding her captive, but it was no use. They wouldn't budge. She and Faith were trapped, and they were going to die.

FOURTEEN

Ben kept an eye on his cell phone as he drove at break-neck speed along the curving road that led up the mountain, thankful for the sturdy vehicle and good tires that kept him from swerving in the wind. He knew this area well, as he had patrolled it many times in the past. There were very few homes in this remote area, but there were a few vacation cabin rentals sprinkled along this road.

He rounded a curve and stared in disbelief at Hannah's car approaching. He leaned toward the windshield to get a better look and gasped in surprise at the sight of Wes and Julie Allen in the front seat. He didn't see Hannah and Faith. Wes must have seen him at that time because Ben had a glimpse of the man's mouth moving as if shouting at Julie before he swerved onto a narrow road that branched off to the right. Ben knew that road. It was rough, steep and dangerous. It wasn't a good exit down the mountain, especially in this weather.

He glanced down at his cell phone and frowned. Faith's GPS didn't show movement. According to what he was seeing, she was trapped in one spot. Despite the temptation to follow Wes and Julie, he knew his only choice was to press on toward Hannah and Faith's location. He accelerated toward the spot marked on the GPS. The thought that he might find their bodies slipped into his mind, and he immediately pushed it away. They couldn't be dead. He had to tell Hannah how much he loved her and how he wanted them to be a family. A gust of wind hit the car at that moment, and he gripped the steering wheel tighter.

Another glance at his cell phone let him know he was approaching a turnoff. He guided his car down the narrow path and screeched to a stop in front of a mountain cabin. His heart plummeted to the pit of his stomach at the scene before his eyes.

Fire leaped up the side of the cabin and was beginning to creep across the roof. With a strangled cry he jumped from the car and ran toward the building. Hannah and Faith were inside, and he had to get to them.

Please, God, he prayed as he ran. *Let them be alive.*

Just as he reached the door a hard wind whipped down from the mountain. Sparks from the flames flew in all directions, and he ducked to keep from being hit. Out of the corner of his eye he could see fire now igniting in the forest beside the cabin. He'd seen wildfires, but he'd never been so close to one before now. Tongues of fire leaped from tree to tree and along the vegetation on the forest floor as the forest burst into flame.

He reached the door and turned the knob, but it wouldn't open. It was locked, and there was no key in the door. He drew back, and with all his might kicked the door, but it refused to open. Panicked now, Ben drew his gun from his holster and fired several shots until the lock pulled free of the door. Then he kicked it again, and it burst open.

Smoke greeted him as he ran inside, but he saw Hannah and Faith right away. They were tied in chairs, and he couldn't tell if they were unconscious from the smoke or already dead. He held his breath and ran to Hannah. Her head lolled back on the chair, but she opened her eyes enough to take in the sight of him. Stark relief filled her face as she told him, "Faith first."

He nodded, picked Faith and the chair up, and rushed out the door. He set her down and ran back inside to Hannah. Again he picked up the chair with her in it and ran from the burning cabin.

When he got back to where he had set Faith down, she was awake and coughing. He pulled out his pocketknife and cut the ropes holding her to the chair and then turned to release Hannah. When she was freed, she reached for Faith, and the girl collapsed in her mother's arms.

Ben turned and stared at the fire that had now spread farther. The forest beside the house was burning as far as he could see. Smoke filled the air, making it difficult to breath. He grabbed Hannah by the arm. "Get up! We've got to get out of here!"

He pulled her up and grabbed Faith up into his arms. He could see that Hannah was having trouble walking. He ran ahead, put Faith in the car and hurried back for Hannah. Lifting her into his arms, he carried her to the car and helped her get inside. Then he ran around to the driver's side and jumped in.

When he pulled the car to a stop at the end of the path that led to the cabin, he stopped and surveyed the scene before him. The wind had increased, and it was whipping sparks back and forth across the road that wound back down the mountain. As he watched, trees on either side of the road erupted like Roman candles and spewed hot sparks in all directions.

Suddenly a small tree on fire crashed across the road, blocking his intended route. At that moment his cell phone rang. Luke's name showed up on caller ID. He connected the call right away.

"Luke, where are you?"

"According to my GPS, I'm probably about a quarter of a mile from you, but either side of the road ahead is burning. The wind is spreading the fire like a blowtorch. There are several trees that look like they're about to topple. Firefighters are on the way. What about Hannah and Faith?"

"I have them, but there's a tree already fallen in our path, and it's blocking our way. The fire seems to be spreading quicker in your direction. You need to turn around and get back down the mountain before you get trapped up here."

"What about you?"

"I can't get down the way I came. There's only one thing for me to do. I'm going to have to go up the mountain. Once I get to the top, I can head down into a valley with a road that leads to the interstate. I may be able to outrun the fire, but you get to safety now."

"Okay, Ben. I'll be praying for you."

"Thanks."

He disconnected the call and looked over at Hannah. Her eyes were big, and she licked her lips. "Ben…"

He reached over and squeezed her hand. "Don't worry. We're going to get out of here." He looked over at Faith in the back seat. He wished he had a car seat for her, but the seat belt he'd buckled her into would have to do. "Hold on tight, honey. We're about to take a wild ride."

Having said that, he turned the car toward the top of the mountain and raced to escape before the fire reached them. *Keep my hands steady on the wheel, Lord. Hannah and Faith have endured too much to die now.*

As Ben careened up the mountain road, he glanced in the rearview mirror from time to time to see the progress of the fire. The wind was blowing the flames down the mountain, and it didn't seem to be spreading very quickly this way. None of them spoke as they sped along to the top of the mountain road and descended to the valley below.

Once they reached the bottom of the mountain, Ben sighed in relief and headed toward the interstate. The fire didn't appear to be threatening their town yet, so he could get on the interstate and have Hannah and Faith at the hospital soon.

He glanced over his shoulder at Faith who sat slumped in the back seat, and his heart lurched. She had coughed all the way down the mountain, and she needed medical help right away. Hannah did, too, but from one glance at her, he could see that she was more worried about Faith than she was about herself.

Ben pulled onto the interstate and turned his siren and blue lights on as he increased his speed. This was an emergency. He had to get them to the hospital as quickly as possible. He pulled out his cell phone and punched the speed dial number for his office. Clara answered right away.

"Ben? Are you all right?"

"Yes, I'm on the way to the hospital with Hannah and Faith. Call the hospital and tell them I have two victims who are suffering from smoke inhalation. They need to have two gurneys waiting at the emergency entrance."

"Got it."

The call disconnected and he raced on.

A few minutes later he pulled into the hospital parking lot and screeched to a stop at the emergency-room entrance. Nurses and several orderlies rushed from the building pushing the two gurneys he'd requested. Before he could get out of the car and come around to the other side, they had Hannah and Faith each on a gurney and were rushing them inside. All he could do was park his car and run back to the entrance.

Once in the waiting room he stopped at the receptionist's desk. She knew him from previous visits to interview victims and their families. "Sheriff Whitman, are you with the two patients who were just brought in?"

"I am. Tell the doctor as soon as he's finished examining them, I'd like to see them."

She nodded. "I'll tell him."

He turned and started toward a chair to take a seat.

Before he could reach it, his cell phone rang. It was his office. "Hello."

"Ben," Luke said. "You made it all right."

"Yeah. How about you? Any trouble?"

"No, but I called to tell you that 911 just got a call about a man and woman stranded on a mountain road. Evidently it's one that branches off that main road we were on. They're at the top on something like an over-look area, and the fire's all around them. The helicopter is getting ready to go rescue them."

Ben's heart gave a small thump. "Did you get their names?"

"Yeah. It's Wes and Julie Allen."

"Tell the helicopter to pick me up at the hospital landing pad. I want to ride along with them."

"Why? Do you know these people?"

Ben chuckled. "Oh, yeah. Take a look at the paper-work on my desk, and you'll understand. I'm on my way to the landing pad."

He disconnected the call and rushed back over to the receptionist. "Tell Mrs. Riley that I had an emergency, but I'll be back as soon as I can."

She nodded, and he turned and ran from the building. He could hear the helicopter already approaching. He stopped and waited until the pilot had landed, then ducked his head and ran toward the chopper. Within minutes he was strapped in, and they were lifting off.

Ben sat back and smiled. He could hardly wait to see the look on Wes's and Julie's faces when he arrested them for kidnapping and attempted murder, and this time he had the evidence to prove it.

* * *

Hannah lay in the hospital bed, her arms wrapped around her daughter. After the doctor had finished his exam of the two of them, Hannah had insisted that the nurses let her lie in the bed with Faith. She'd almost lost her precious daughter today, and right now she wanted to touch her and convince herself that they had really escaped that burning cabin. But they wouldn't have if it hadn't been for Ben.

The memory of him bursting through the door and carrying them to safety returned, and she smiled. She had little recollection of their wild ride down the mountain during which she'd drifted in and out of consciousness, but she knew he had driven as if his car had wings and had gotten them to the hospital as quickly as he could.

The doctor had assured her that they were both going to be all right. No permanent damage had been done, and after a few breathing treatments he would be sending them home. All would be perfect right now if she knew where Ben was. The emergency-room receptionist had relayed a message from him that he'd had to leave for an emergency, but that he'd be back. That had been several hours ago, and she was starting to worry. What if he'd had to go back into the fire area and had been hurt?

She pushed the thought from her mind. If he'd been hurt, he would have been brought here, and surely someone would have told her. Patience. That's what she needed. He would be back.

She lay there stroking Faith's hair and snuggling

closer to her. It still scared her how close they'd come to dying, but the important thing was that they hadn't. She had to keep remembering that.

Suddenly she stilled at the sound of footsteps coming down the hall. She'd know that stride anywhere. Ben had returned.

A knock sounded at the door. She swallowed and flinched at how raw her throat felt. "Come in." It came out like a whisper, and she was surprised he could even hear her.

The door opened, and he walked in. Soot stained his clothes, but she didn't care. He was the best sight she'd seen in a long time. He stood just inside the room and stared at her. "Hi," he said.

"Hi," she whispered back.

She had promised herself that she wouldn't cry, but her resolve to be brave suddenly dissolved, and she began to sob. He was at her side instantly and grabbed her hand.

"What's wrong? Are you in pain?"

She bit down on her lip and shook her head. "N-No," she stuttered. "I-I'm just so thankful that you found us. I thought we were going to die, and then you were there."

He wiped the tears from her cheeks. "Don't cry. Everything's all right now. You and Faith are safe, and the doctor says you're going to be fine."

"Thanks to you." She smiled through her tears and stared up at him. "You have a smudge on your cheek and soot on your clothes. How did that happen?"

He reached behind him with his free hand and

pulled a chair closer to the bed. "I went back to the fire."

"What?" she cried. Faith stirred in her arms, and she lowered her voice. "Why did you go back?"

"We got a call that there were some people stranded up on the mountain. I went with the mountain rescue patrol in the helicopter."

"Did you get them back safely?"

He smiled. "Yeah, but they weren't too happy to see me when I got off that chopper."

"Why not?"

His smile turned into a laugh. "Because it was Wes and Julie Allen. They made a big mistake with the road they took to escape. The fire spread that way and stranded them at an overlook. But I was glad to see them. It gave me great pleasure to put handcuffs on both of them and escort them to jail, which is where they are residing now."

She breathed a sigh of relief. "I'm so glad you caught them." A sudden thought crossed her mind, and she frowned. "But what about Chuck Murray?"

Ben shrugged. "What can I say? I was wrong about him. I apologized and released him from custody." He paused a moment and grinned. "I did, however, suggest that he might be happier living somewhere else. I have a feeling he won't be asking for any more lessons."

A lighthearted laugh bubbled up in her throat. "Oh, Ben, you're wonderful."

A somber expression covered his face. "No, you're the wonderful one. I've always known that."

She held her breath as he leaned over and touched

his forehead to hers. He closed his eyes for a moment and clasped her hand tighter. "I was so scared," he whispered. "When I saw that fire, I thought I hadn't gotten to you in time, and I knew if anything happened to you and Faith, I would have nothing left in my world that truly mattered to me."

"Don't think like that now. You did make it in time, and we're all right."

He pulled back and stared down at her. "I was afraid I wouldn't get to say the words."

Her forehead wrinkled. "What words?"

He smiled and brushed a strand of hair away from her forehead. "I love you, Hannah Riley. I've loved you since the day I saw you get out of that car at your grandfather's house. I should have told you years ago before you met Shane, but I didn't think I was worthy of you. I didn't tell you how I felt, and you married a man who caused you so much suffering. If I had told you back then, things might have been different."

She shook her head. "We can't undo the past, Ben. Now we have to find a way to go forward. You've been so good to me through the years, the best friend I've ever had. And I think that's the basis for a strong relationship. You can't love someone unless they're your friend, and I love you, Ben Whitman. I have for some time now."

He pulled her hand to his lips and grazed kisses across her knuckles. "I've been so blind. I used an excuse from the past to convince myself that I would fail you, and almost missed out on the chance to be with you. I know I can't promise to always get everything right, but I'll try my best to never fail you or Faith."

She smiled. "You didn't fail us today." She glanced down at Faith who was still sleeping. "We're all here, all three of us, and I think God has lots of wonderful blessings waiting for us."

His eyes sparkled. "I think so, too. The first thing I want is to get your answer to a question."

"What question?"

His Adam's apple bobbed. "Hannah Riley, will you do me the honor of becoming my wife?"

A tear slipped from the corner of her eye. "I would be honored to be your wife, Ben Whitman."

He smiled and then lowered his lips to hers. "I love you," he whispered, and the words fanned her lips. "I'll never grow tired of telling you that."

"I'll never grow tired of hearing it."

Then he pressed his lips to hers, and her heart pounded. This was what she had wanted. This was what she needed.

He pulled away and sat there letting his gaze drift over her face. He glanced down at Faith as she stirred in Hannah's arms. She opened her eyes and smiled when she saw Ben. "Hi, Ben," she whispered.

Moisture filled his eyes, and he blinked. "Hi, sweetheart, how are you feeling?"

"My throat hurts a little."

He reached over and patted her arm. "It will get better. I'll see to it. When the doctor says you can go home, I'll buy you all the ice cream you can eat. Would you like that?"

Her eyebrows shot up. "Yes," she croaked, the sound revealing how much her throat hurt. She lay there for a minute and stared at him before she smiled. "I knew you would come for us. I told Mommy not to be scared, that you would save us. And I was right."

"You don't ever have to worry. I'll take care of you forever."

She smiled once more and then snuggled close to Hannah and drifted off to sleep again. Hannah looked up at him. "She loves you, Ben."

"And I love her, too. I want us to give her a home with a mother and father."

She grinned. "And maybe some brothers and sisters?"

He laughed. "That sounds like a winner to me."

Then he lowered his mouth and captured hers again. Her heart soared, and she said a silent prayer of thanks for bringing them to each other.

Hannah stood in the entry hall of their church and thought of all that had happened in the last three months since Ben had rescued her and Faith. They'd been able to make it to Korea after all in plenty of time for the competition, and she'd come home with a first place finish in Fast Shot and a second place finish in Single Shot. By the time they'd returned home, the wildfire had long been extinguished and life was moving on in the Smokies.

Now the day she'd been waiting for had arrived. Any second now she would hear the first notes of the "Bridal Chorus" and she would walk down the aisle to become Ben's wife. Faith fidgeted in her lace dress and shifted from foot to foot, impatient to get on with it. Hannah felt the same way. She couldn't contain her happiness. Dusty stood at her side, ready to escort her in and give her away. She knew her grandfather would be pleased that Dusty was doing that honor.

The music began, and she looked at Dusty. "Are you ready?"

He held out his arm, and she slipped hers through his. "You look beautiful today, Hannah. I wish your grandfather was here to see you."

Tears pricked her eyes, but she couldn't cry, not today of all days. She took a deep breath. The wedding planner stepped to the door, opened it and smiled down at Faith. "Don't forget to scatter your rose petals."

Faith nodded and moved slowly down the aisle, just as they had practiced last night. Hannah gave Dusty one last glance, and then they stepped out behind her daughter. Hannah's eyes scanned the guests who had come today.

She and Ben had decided they wanted a small wedding with just the special people in their lives in attendance, and that's who had come. Dean Harwell stood next to Ben at the front, their eyes glued to her. Dean's wife, Gwen, and daughter, Maggie, sat in the second row beside Luke Conrad and his wife, Cheyenne. Maria sat behind them next to Gabriel Decker and his wife, Liz. They had come all the way from Texas to see the man Gabriel had become close friends with get married. On the other side of the aisle Clara sat with all the deputies and their families.

For the first time in years, she felt like she was enveloped with love, and she smiled at the man who had brought happiness back into her life. He didn't look away, and neither did she. They had eyes only for each other today, and for all days to come.

When she and Dusty reached the front of the church and Dusty had handed her off to Ben, she leaned toward Ben and whispered in his ear. "I love you, Ben Whitman, till death us do part."

His eyes shone with love for her, and he whispered back, "Till death us do part."

Then they turned and faced the pastor. Ben squeezed her hand tighter as he began to recite his vows. Hannah heard the words. She knew what they were promising each other, but for now all she wanted was to remember the way Ben looked at her when he said, "I, Ben, take you, Hannah, to be my wedded wife to have and to hold from this day forward."

* * * * *

Be sure to pick up the other stories in
SMOKY MOUNTAIN SECRETS:

IN A KILLER'S SIGHTS
STALKING SEASON
RANCH HIDEOUT

Find more great reads at www.LoveInspired.com

Dear Reader,

I hope you enjoyed reading *Point Blank*. The idea for this book is a result of my daughter's interest in mounted archery. It is a sport that combines excellent horsemanship with the accuracy of archery. Perseverance in learning these skills is of vital importance if someone expects to excel in this sport. So it is in life. Each day we must persevere if we are to live the life that God expects of us. Sometimes the mistakes we've made in our pasts come back to remind us of what we once were, but Jesus's teachings tell us that we must always look to the future and put away those things that are behind us. We must press on as if we are in a race and are determined to win. If you haven't accepted this attitude in your life, I pray that you will. He is waiting to give you the peace you're seeking.

Sandra Robbins

Get 2 Free Books,
Plus 2 Free Gifts—
just for trying the Reader Service!

Austin stepped closer to her. "I think this is personal,
Kylie. Someone wants you dead."

Mercedes stopped crying. Her soft fingers brushed over
Kylie's neck as she grabbed her collar to hold on to. While
a thousand conflicting emotions tumbled through Kylie's
mind, the only clear thought was that she wanted to keep
Mercedes safe. Mercedes stuck two fingers in her mouth
and stared up at Kylie, a look of total trust in her eyes.

"I think you need to put that kid in protective custody so
you can do your job and resolve this threat," Austin said.

Kylie couldn't believe what she was hearing. "So I can
do my job?" Was that what mattered the most to him?

Austin paced. His hand gestures indicated he was rattled. "Both of you could have died out there." What was going on with him, anyway? He was Mr. Cool Under Fire. She'd never seen him this upset.

"I know that. Don't you think I know that?" Kylie wrestled with even more doubt. More than anything she wanted to keep Mercedes safe, but the thought of being separated from her nearly broke her in half. She was the one who could best protect her, and the shots had been fired at her, not at the baby. Was the little girl really in danger if she stayed? Mercedes had lost her mother. Turning her over to strangers would only add trauma on trauma. Her insides twisted from the turmoil she felt. Austin was right, though—something bad could have happened to Mercedes.

He combed his fingers through his dark blond hair. "We need to get Garcia, and we need to get whoever shot at you. Chances are, they're connected."

"We?" Her jaw tightened. It was clear he was uncomfortable with her new status as a single mother. He just wanted her to be Kylie, unattached, trusted border patrol agent, focused on nothing more than the job. But that wasn't her anymore. She was a mother now. Didn't he understand that?

Don't miss
THANKSGIVING PROTECTOR by Sharon Dunn,
available October 2017 wherever
Love Inspired® Suspense books and ebooks are sold.

www.LoveInspired.com